"I Plan To Snare You," Margot Said. "But I Want You Willing."

John stared at her in disbelief. "Hell, woman, I'm about as willing as a man can get."

"For sex. I want love."

"You sure know how to make it hard for a guy," he told her.

"I didn't do anything!" she protested.

"You wore that dress."

"Good grief! That dress isn't wicked. It's a perfectly decent dress!" She got out of the bed, went over to the closet and took out the dress. She spread it over her pajamas and frowned at him, annoyed. "It's perfectly okay!"

"You're right. It's your body that's the scandal."

"Baloney!" Standing in the flannel pajamas, she held out her arms and said, "See?"

Smoldering on the bed, he suggested, "Come back to bed. You'll catch cold out there."

And darned if she didn't crawl right back in with him....

Dear Reader,

Happy New Year! The New Year means new beginnings, a renewed sense of purpose. It also means New Year resolutions, and I have one I want to share with all of you.

I resolve to continue to bring you the sexiest, sassiest, most sparkling love stories around. In the upcoming year, you'll see books both from new authors and your special favorites. These writers are committed to creating wonderful romances filled with love and laughter, tears and joys, and to inventing heroes who will fulfill your every fantasy.

I also resolve to continue to publish books filled with variety. Six Desire books are available for you each and every month, and you, as readers, should expect that the stories have difference and diversity. So expect a fabulous mix of traditional stories and bold, innovative plot lines.

Silhouette Desire is ever-changing and ever-challenging. But the one thing that will never change is its quality. I thank you all for your continued support throughout the years, because without the readers there wouldn't be Silhouette Desire!

Sincerely,

Lucia Macro
Silhouette Desire

Please address questions and book requests to:
Reader Service
U.S.: P.O. Box 1325, Buffalo, NY 14269
Canadian: P.O. Box 1050, Niagara Falls, Ont. L2E 7G7

LASS
SMALL
A NEW YEAR

SILHOUETTE *Desire*®

Published by Silhouette Books

America's Publisher of Contemporary Romance

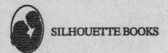 SILHOUETTE BOOKS

ISBN 0-373-05830-6

A NEW YEAR

Printed in U.S.A.

Books by Lass Small

Silhouette Desire

Tangled Web #241
To Meet Again #322
Stolen Day #341
Possibles #356
Intrusive Man #373
To Love Again #397
Blindman's Bluff #413
*Goldilocks and the Behr #437
*Hide and Seek #453
*Red Rover #491
*Odd Man Out #505
*Tagged #534
Contact #548
Wrong Address, Right Place #569
Not Easy #578
The Loner #594
Four Dollars and Fifty-One Cents #613
*No Trespassing Allowed #638
The Molly Q #655
†'Twas the Night #684
*Dominic #697
†A Restless Man #731
†Two Halves #743
†Beware of Widows #755
A Disruptive Influence #775
†Balanced #800
†Tweed #817
†A New Year #830

Silhouette Romance

An Irritating Man #444
Snow Bird #521

Silhouette Books

Silhouette Christmas Stories 1989
"Voice of the Turtles"
Silhouette Spring Fancy 1993
"Chance Encounter"

*Lambert Series
†Fabulous Brown Brothers

LASS SMALL

finds living on this planet at this time a fascinating experience. People are amazing. She thinks that to be a teller of tales of people, places and things is absolutely marvelous.

To all the New Years
and to hope for
this world in a
tough time

One

It all began just before the new year. John Brown had gone with his boss, Lemon Covington, over to San Antonio on business. John was Lemon's financial adviser and good friend.

The two men were very similar, but there were differences. While both men were tall and well built, John was about two inches shorter than Lemon and his hair was a darker blond. Additionally, John was an observer while Lemon was a participator.

On that day, they were in the conference room of an office suite with some hard-sell manipulators who wanted Covington's money for speculation.

Almost totally silent, John sat, listening, his expressions concealed by his long eyelashes and short, neat beard. He listened and made notes.

The speculators had been "selling" to both men, but there must have been something about John's rare glance and hard eyes that had diverted their attentions to concentrate on the more affable Lemon.

With the afternoon sun lowering in the sky, Lemon had declined to be hurried into any decision. The two victims rose, so the vultures had to stand, too.

Stretching, saying nothing important, Lemon and John left the wheeler-dealers high and dry, assuring them their premise would be considered.

Exiting the building, John said, "They're rattlesnakes."

Lemon agreed. "Yeah. But it *was* interesting. I like seeing how such men operate. It's a thing to learn. I'm sure glad I have the trust fund."

"Yes." John was looking off down the street.

It was then that Lemon studied John through narrowed, considering eyes. He was concerned for John. And he made up his mind. He said, "Hey, John. We gotta go down the street. I have ta get something."

They went to a big posh store by the Menger Hotel on Alamo Plaza, and the people there laughed out loud when Lemon hollered, "Here I am! Watch out, now, or I'll fool you into giving it to me."

Lemon was one hell of a bargainer. The surprise was that he made dealing such fun—and he was so nice about it—that people thought they'd done okay, anyway.

So did John.

After Lemon had been shown all sorts of women's clothing, from riding habits to cocktail gowns, he bought a scandalous spangly RED dress. It made a small package.

They retrieved Lemon's car, which had cost the price of a medium-size house, and they went to a neighborhood in the northeastern part of the city.

Lemon parked by the curb in front of a medium-size house. As he got out of the car, he said to John, "I'll be right back." Then he went along the walk carrying the package up the steps to the porch, where he knocked on the door.

John looked around the middle-class neighborhood. It wasn't one that Lemon would frequent. It was staid.

The door opened, and a young woman stood talking to Lemon. She pushed away the package he offered her. She shook her head. She laughed. She wouldn't take the red dress.

Lemon called, "John! Could you come here a minute, please?"

See? Lemon asked favors. He never directed or commanded or ordered. He was a gentle man. A strange man, but a thoughtful one who was gentle.

John didn't want to meet the woman.

What was John supposed to do, say "No" and just sit there? Anyway, he was curious to see the woman who wouldn't take the dress from Lemon.

As the couple on the porch waited, watching John, he slowly exited the car and looked around as he closed the car door. Then he, too, went along the walk and up the steps to the porch.

In the do-you-understand way of Texans, Lemon said, "Margot, this is John Brown? No, really, that's his name. He's from Ohio. I bet you knew right away that he wasn't Texan."

John saw a pretty young woman with a laughing face, earrings and long, careless brown hair. Her eyes were blue. She was wearing jeans and a shirt with the sleeves rolled up. She looked like any other pretty woman.

For her edification, Lemon reasoned with John, "She thinks I'm after her body, which is a logical assumption, and that I'm giving her this dress to wear at my party because I have ulterior motives. Explain it all to her."

John shrugged and lied, "Lemon is having a 'must' party for a bunch of people he owes invitations, and he desperately needs at least one guest there who doesn't want anything from him and who's there just to have a good time."

Lemon said, "Exactly." And he smiled at the woman.

She asked John, "Are you going?"

"I doubt it."

Lemon countered, "He's in the depths of despair and doesn't believe he should be at a party at this time."

"Why?"

"Tell her, John."

"I have Mr. Covington for a boss."

She laughed in delight.

John went back to the car, reclined the seat and lay back, but his eyes slid over and kept track of his boss and the woman who wouldn't let Lemon inside her house. Interesting.

Lemon stood on the porch and talked and talked and talked. He sure was a talker. Lemon was such a talker that a man found himself doing the damnedest things. John gave a single, impressed, minute shake of his head and sighed, just thinking of the things Lemon had talked HIM into doing.

Once they'd coaxed a wild dog to eat from their hands. They'd hung off a trestle as a train went over it. They'd ridden a bull who'd preferred being with a cow. All were stupid things.

But just recalling that made John wonder about the women in Lemon's life. What did he talk *them* into doing?

Eventually, Lemon came back and got into the car without the package. He could talk a woman into anything.

As much as Lemon irritated and exasperated John, as much as he tried to keep Lemon from frittering all his means away, John had acknowledged to himself that Lemon was a shrewd operator. He had known Lemon for four years now, and he was only just beginning to understand that Lemon had been testing and training him all that while. And the man was only a year older than John. It rankled him that Lemon could be only a year older and that much smarter.

So, on New Year's Eve, there was John Brown, third adopted son of Salty Brown of Temple, Ohio, at a party on an aptly named Cactus Ridge in West Texas. He didn't know why he'd allowed himself to be convinced that it was his duty to attend...and to wear a tuxedo.

Hell.

Lemon's house was out on the edge of forever. You could look out in any direction and not see anything but TEXAS. There were mesquite trees, a couple of oaks, a lot of winter-dried Johnson grass and probably an equal amount of cacti.

It was all very different from Ohio.

But it was all Lemon's. Yeah, Lemon. What a name. When people questioned how his name had come about, Lemon claimed he'd been named by his parents who took a sour view of him. And that just might not be Lemon talk.

Lemon had received the house from his momma. And his daddy had given him the cash in trust to fund him.

Think of the desperation of the parents who would give a man a house like that and the means to live the way Lemon lived—just to get shed of him!

In spite of his beard, John still looked younger than Lemon, who was only that one single year older. And watching Lemon, John knew—without any question at all—that he would never be able to sweet-talk a woman or convince a man the way Lemon could. It was an art. Probably genetic.

The woman, right over there in the sparkly red dress, was the only one Lemon had had to coax to come there. She was the one who had resisted Lemon's lure on the front porch of her house. She was elusive. She was something. She was laughing and flirting, and she was skimpily dressed. Lemon had bought her that dress.

All the people in that monstrous house were friends to Lemon Covington. They'd come to bid goodbye to the old year and welcome the next one. Some of the crowd were married, but most were loose and acted that way.

And then there was John Brown.

The New Year's Eve party was going full tilt, and the night was still young. Aloof and withdrawn, John watched the guests. He wished he were back at his place with a good book, a glass of brandy, a fire in the fireplace . . . alone.

A waiter came by to refill John's drink, but it was Lemon who gave John a platter of hors d'oeuvres.

Lemon said, "Eat. Eat. I can't have my financial adviser loopy or passing out. People would think they could take advantage of me!"

Take advantage of Lemon Covington? That was just plain silly.

John arranged his stance and face so that he looked at Lemon soberly. And again, it was brought to John's attention that Lemon was a good-looking man. He wasn't a pretty boy, he was a man. He stood tall and straight, but he was never overbearing. John shook his head chidingly, and Lemon laughed as he went away among his guests.

It was a noisy party. The big old house that was set in a sea of mesquite and cacti, out in the middle of nowhere, was stuffed with a fascinating variety of people. They had come for the weekend, and they were all bent on having a good time.

A good time wasn't on John's agenda. He wanted to be alone, grieve for the passing year and maybe get really/really drunk. Oblivion was alluring.

The coming new year wouldn't hold any memory of his ex-lover—Lucilla. His life would be forced to go on beyond. He couldn't ever again think: I saw her last spring. No. It would be: I saw her last year. Then it would be...two years ago. And finally it would be vague as to which spring it had been. Which year.

He didn't want to relinquish her. He didn't want her to be vaguely somewhere in his past. He wanted the memories fresh. As much as they hurt, he wanted the pain because it meant she was still there with him.

John put his glass down on a padded table. He turned away to walk around the edge of the room, past the laughing, talking people, and go down the main cross hall. At the other end of the hall was the library.

The double doors were open. John went inside and closed the doors.

There was a fire in the fireplace. It was the only illumination. The chairs and sofa were large and comfortable. It was an inviting room. He stood and was glad to be alone. There were the books, the paintings and a decanter of brandy with some small glasses. Small. Well, he could refill one. He poured himself a full amount in the limiting bulb of a glass.

He went over to a chair and sat down. He sank back, and his gaze on the fire was unseeing. He saw Lucilla in the flames. How appropriate that she-devil was on fire. Her blond hair shimmered in the winds of the dancing flames, and her body writhed in pulsating undulations. She beckoned to him, and he heard her laugh....

He started up at the sound, but it was only someone passing in the hall.

He looked at the untouched brandy and scowled at it. He threw the liquid into the fire, causing it to sputter and flare. Then he went back to the table and returned the glass to the tray.

Owned by a bachelor, Lemon's house was so large that it was an oddly anonymous dwelling. Mixed with the distant music, John could hear the muted voices of the guests and the laughter, the higher pitch of the women and the rumbling of the men. It sounded like a mob had invaded the place and was enjoying raiding it.

John considered how isolated they were.

He went back to the chair. Then he got up and paced. He went to the window and lifted the drape aside to look out onto the dead night. It was clear.

Gradually he could see the millions and billions of stars.

He wondered at all the planets that had to be around most of those points of light. At incomprehensible distances, what other beings lived and loved and reproduced and suffered, out in the incredibly isolated or perhaps quarantined habitations in space?

There was no way we could be so unique here on this earth. He remembered reading that we were the isolation depot for the galaxy's insane. That sounded reasonable, having witnessed the madness of humankind. But he wasn't one. Why was he there, alive and on this planet?

And he wondered if it was all worthwhile.

He stared glumly, considering that our attempts to contact the other beings beyond our range could well bring on our destruction or enslavement to unimagined creatures.

Someone tried the door. Like a hostile alien himself, John turned his eyes to stare at the door and mentally forbade any invasion of his territory—the library. This peace was his.

Undeterred by his thought shield, the handle turned and the door opened. That sparkly red-dressed woman came inside. As she looked at the chairs and around the room, she closed the door carefully. Apparently the room, with its concealing shadows, appeared empty. She had assumed she was alone. She dropped her shoulders and relaxed, and she locked the door.

She carried a bottle of wine. She went to the tray and noted the brandy glasses and gave a single, derisive sound at the size of the glasses. She poured a taste of the wine and drank it in a gulp. Putting the glass

down, she glanced casually around the room, seeing
it enough.

With only the fire's light, she investigated her recently claimed realm. She walked along slowly, looking at the titles of the books filling the shelves. She
would take a book out and open it, then put it back.
She was curious and interested. She stood and exam-
ined the paintings spaced around the room between
the high sections of shelves filled with books. The
pictures were life-size. One was of Adam and Eve, and
like the others, it was hung at eye level.

She stood and contemplated the painting. Adam
wore a fig leaf. He was heroically male. She leaned
over and looked closer at the fig leaf. Her chuckle was
so amused. Then she reached out a finger and swung
the detached leaf to one side. She laughed a delightful
trill that was very amused.

John frowned. As long as he'd been around Lemon,
he hadn't known that fig leaf was movable. What was
under it to make her laugh? How like Lemon to have
a joke that he never mentioned.

John's unknowing guest then went back to the table, picked up her wine bottle and went toward the
fire. Her silhouette was strongly stirring to a man who
was grieving for a woman lost to him, a man who had
no feelings about this world or its people.

She moved to John's side of the fireplace, and he
could see through the spangles. He would bet good
money that she wasn't wearing anything else. Well, she
had on shoes but nothing else. He was sure. How
could he be so affected by this female?

He'd met her earlier at her house. Her name was
Margot Pulver, and she was Lemon's woman. She was
out-of-bounds for John. It had been Lemon who'd

bought her that outrageous red dress. Held up at the store, on a hanger, it hadn't seemed so wicked.

Why had she intruded into his space here in the library? What if she'd arranged to meet Lemon here? Why here? They both had rooms in the house. They had no reason to meet in the library.

She moved around. While the glittering cloth peaked at the tips of her breasts, the silhouette showed the exact formation of those soft, hidden delights. She turned her body, warming it by the fire.

He watched her as she tilted up the bottle and took a gulp. She pulled up her shoulders and shivered. First she belched and then she sneezed.

Not a drinker.

John shifted his feet and waited for her to see him. He was obstinate about speaking first. She had invaded his bastion.

He had not objected.

Well, to people who have been invited as weekend guests, a library in a house could well be considered common ground.

He looked at her shadowed body in that spangled nothing dress. He might tolerate her to be there for a while. The door was locked. No one else could enter. She thought she was alone. He smiled behind his beard.

She shivered in the heat and turned again. As she lifted the bottle to take another sip, she saw him. His dark tux in the shadows made his face appear to float in the dark. She lowered the bottle and stared, her lips parted. He felt a squiggle in his sex that was urgent.

She said, "Well, John, so here you are. I thought you'd left."

"How do you suppose I'd get through that locked door?"

"I give up."

He was so caught by those appropriate words, that he couldn't remember the conversation.

She asked, "You're able to walk through doors, walls? You appear solid."

"Of course." He was completely concentrated on her, trying to figure out why she so entranced him. He'd never before understood men who could be affected by a strange woman who really did nothing to attract them. He was beginning to understand.

However, she *had* done something to attract attention. She'd worn that spangled, web dress without anything under it. Just her. And she'd slid Adam's fig leaf aside.

He told her, "You ought to wear underwear."

"I beg your pardon!"

He missed her put-down. He nodded in accepting her apology. He said, "For a woman to run around mostly naked the—" And his mind forgot words and just concentrated on the fact that she was so nearly naked.

She looked down at her chest. "Mostly naked?" She was huffy. "I am not, either! You're hallucinating. I'm decently covered."

"I can see your body."

"You have X-ray eyes?"

"No. I can see through that material."

"Good heavens. You're a lecher!"

"I am not! I'm a decent man, and you're a hot woman who is careless with her body."

"Why, you stupid creature!"

"You ought to go put on some clothes."

"I have on all the clothing I can wear under this dress. What I have on, under this dress, is my business and not yours. You ought to keep your filthy mind to yourself! To think that I came here so that I could see you! I have never been so insulted in all of my life. And no man has ever spoken to me as you're speaking. You can dry up and blow away!"

She flung out an arm. Her breasts jiggled and her hair flung and she looked furious and—quite enchanting. He realized he was out in left field and he'd better start backtracking. He said, "I suppose you aren't aware that the dress is transparent." He gestured to show he was only being kind to impart the information.

"Go stick your head in a barrel."

But she didn't leave. He gestured to the door. "You could leave, you know. All you have to do is unl—"

"I was here first. I don't know how you got in here, but you just get yourself out of here, however you did that, and don't speak to me." She folded her arms across her nice breasts and bounced angrily on her heels, which shimmied her bottom. She was wonderful.

Slowly, searching for words, he said, "Uhh, I apologize."

She looked at him in astonishment. "You mean you admit you lied?"

"No. I'm sorry I mentioned anything that would upset you."

She jabbed her thumb over her shoulder and commanded, "Out."

With a man-in-control voice, he warned, "If you don't settle down, I won't save you when the aliens invade and wipe out all of civilization."

She observed him clinically. "Are you working with a full deck?"

"I was looking outside—"

In an unbelieving voice, she supplied, "And you saw them land."

He asked with some interest, "You knew they were coming?"

"Yeah. Sure."

He moved to the table with studied care. "Would you like a brandy?"

"No."

"More wine?"

"You're trying to make up."

"Yeah."

"Admit you were just being nasty when you said my dress is transparent."

"Uhh..." He looked down her body. Then he took a steadying breath and again just said, "Uhh..."

Being obvious about it, she inhaled a deep, impatient breath.

He put his hand to his head. "I suppose about the only thing that's going to calm me down is if you allow me to make love to you."

"Love!"

"Couple?" He was helpful.

She dismissed him. "I can't believe you're real. In the brief time back when I met you, you seemed like a logical, controlled, placid man." She stated that with carefully enunciated words.

"When was that?"

"When you and Lemon delivered this dress to my house."

John nodded once, slowly. As he tried to think of the right words, he licked around the lower edge of the mustache of his beard, feeling the bristled ends of the trimmed hair with the tip of his tongue.

She guessed. "It was you who just landed. This is an invasion like the *Body Snatchers,* and you've taken over John Brown's body. You don't remember meeting me at all because you weren't there. What have you done with John?"

John laughed.

She relaxed a little and said, "So, what are your plans for the world?"

"Complete restructuring."

She considered that. "It could use some help, but you've got a real problem with dresses. This is a perfectly decent dress. I'm covered."

"With gauze."

"This is not a bandage. This is a dress. *D-r-e-s-s.* That's what women wear. Men wear suits. You have one on. Mine is not transparent." She looked down him. "You are a little obvious. Do you understand the body you're in?" Before he could reply, she went quickly on, "Do you understand about eating and sleeping?"

In measured words, he replied, "We do neither. It seems wasteful, but there's something called *s-e-x* that sounds strange and puzzling. What's that all about?"

"I believe you need to go back to the manual."

"I can only hold this body for a limited time. Our respiration is different. I am beginning to pant. I shall see you at another time, and you can demonstrate the *s-e-x* part." He put his hand to his head and wobbled a little. Then he asked in a dazed manner, "What happened? Who are you? Oh. Margot?"

"Well done." She bobbed her head with the words. "Quick." She nodded some more. "I don't believe

I've ever seen an alien intrusion that was so smoothly done."

"You're mistaken. It was I who was intruded upon. Where did you come from? The last I knew, I was sitting in front of the fire. When did you come in?"

"If you don't remember when I came in, how do you know you were invaded by an alien?"

"An *alien?* Someone from across the border or someone from outer space?"

She was patient. "Space."

"Well, I'll be darned."

"Do you have theatrical blood in your family?"

He considered his adoptive mother, Felicia. "Not directly, why?"

"You're really quite brilliant."

"I'll tell my mother that, and she'll be pleased."

"Aliens have mothers?" She rather exaggerated her surprise. "I thought they hatched."

"Somebody lays the eggs. Or releases the pods or whatever."

"How do you know that?"

He shrugged. "It's logical."

"Didn't Mr. Spock always say that?"

"I believe he did."

"Let me see your ears."

He felt them first, then said, "I believe they're all right again. Were they pointed while the 'other' was in me?"

"I couldn't tell."

"Come sit down by the fire...no, here on the sofa. There. I feel somewhat unsettled. May I put my head on your lap?" He gingerly went ahead and did that.

He sighed, and with great discretion looked past her breasts to her face. "Now tell me what all I said when you arrived and the 'other' had possession of me."

Two

Margot looked down over her chest at John whose head was on her lap, uninvited, and she asked, "Just what are you doing with your head on my lap?"

He looked back up over that same nice chest and replied, "You're being a good Samaritan."

"Oh?" Her question was doubtful. Very doubtful.

"I've just experienced an intrusion by a space alien. He took over my consciousness, my voice box and my body. You've been very supportive."

"In what way?"

"Well." He searched frantically around in his mind and didn't find one damned thing. He suggested, "You believed me."

She replied, "Hah!"

He chided gently, "That sounds as if you aren't entirely certain that this remarkable contact by an alien did actually occur."

"That is a very understandable assumption."

His tongue ran along his upper lip, touching along the edge of his mustache. "It did occur."

"I have only your word."

"It isn't my word! It was *your* experience. As I understand the exchange, he was after an experience in s-e-x. Wasn't he suggesting that during the time in which you were objecting to his rude references to your—uh—transparent garment?"

"How would you know that?"

He put his hand to his forehead and his fingers brushed against the underside of her breast. "Oops, sorry. The intrusion is hazy... I'm not entirely sure. Perhaps a portion of my consciousness was needed for my body to function so that I wouldn't die of terror?"

"Quick." She nodded in self-agreement. "You are quick, I'll give you that."

He guessed, "You don't actually believe in the space alien?"

"You manage another 'brushing' and I'll eliminate your voice box."

"Wow! Have you been invaded, too? I've never heard such rough talk from a...lady."

"In self-preservation, ladies have learned that they don't have to put up with 'accidental' brushings or sly hanky-panky."

"Oh, are those current wordages?"

"Are you slipping back into the alien's control?"

He looked at her with candor. "What...alien?"

She sighed, and he got to watch from an advantageous angle. She said in a gritty voice, "You get off my lap, or I'll smash your Adam's apple."

He sat up in a slow, thoughtful way and looked back at her over his shoulder. "That's from the Bible. The guilty Adam couldn't swallow the bit of apple with which Eve had tempted him."

She demurred. "Adam handed Eve the apple as he choked on his bite when God said, 'Ah-HAH!' The guilty bite got caught in Adam's throat, and men have borne that mark of evasiveness ever since."

He said as if in rote, "That isn't in the manual."

"You probably have the male version."

He rubbed his nose hard so that he wouldn't laugh. "What did you see when you shifted the fig leaf off Adam's genitals?"

She gasped.

He clarified his question, "I saw you."

"I don't care to discuss this at all. It's none of your business."

"Do you know I've been in and out of this house for four years and I never knew Adam had a movable fig leaf?"

She was aloof. . . and unresponsive.

He pressed, "What's under the fig leaf?"

She looked off into the shadows, and tilting her head forty-five different ways, she refused to reply.

He put his feet on the floor and sighed. "I suppose I'll have to go over and move the fig leaf. And I'll be disappointed."

She said nothing.

"I remember once being in a bar and everyone watched the ladies' room door. I commented to the bartender that it seemed a juvenile occupation. He explained, 'There's a painting of Adam and Eve in the ladies' rest room.'

"I asked if there was a blindfold over Adam's eyes? And the bartender said, 'No. But he's wearing a fig leaf and there's a sign that tells the ladies: Do not lift the fig leaf.' He didn't go on with the story, so I encouraged him, 'And—

"'And an elegant lady went into the room alone. She saw the sign and lifted the fig leaf.' The bartender smiled at me and enjoyed the pause. Then he said, 'Bells blasted, whistles blew, it was pandemonium! She opened the door to find herself spotlighted, and there were cheers and whistles and drumrolls.'"

Margot speculated, "She never went back."

John inquired, "Aren't you curious what she saw?"

Margot squinted her eyes and guessed, "An alarm system?"

His eyes held laughter, but he then coaxed, "What did you see under this Adam's fig leaf?" He indicated the painting.

She gestured, "What sort of a surprise do you think it could be?"

"Tell me."

"Go see for yourself!"

"I don't want to look at painted genitals."

She tucked her lower lip under her upper teeth in order to hide her smile, but her eyes flickered lights of humor.

He speculated, "It's some sort of joke."

She shrugged indifferently and said again, "Go look."

"You laughed."

"I'm not sure we have similar humors."

He eyed her. Her comment implied that he had no humor at all. He stood up and stretched. He asked civilly, "Would you like a brandy?"

"I still have my wine."

"That's an interesting name for a wine. *Alle?* What vineyard?"

"California alleys?" Her look was all candor.

He again took a slow, steadying breath. Then he poured himself a shot of brandy. One never drank brandy by "shots" because that would be unthinkably crass. One sipped brandy. He sipped from the small glass. And across the way, he looked at the shadowed Adam, who appeared to watch John with the patient eyes of an adult.

John inquired with studied interest, "Did the gift of that dress convince you to come to the party?"

"No." She contemplated the fire.

"Why are you here? Are you Lemon's new woman?"

"No."

John frowned at her. "How come you're here then?"

She shrugged, moving the dress-material's sparklies in a dancing way, calling attention to her chest. But she continued to gaze at the fire.

And he recalled that she'd said she'd come there to see—him. Why? He considered her in a very speculative manner. What did she want of him? Any woman would choose Lemon over John Brown. Was she using him to tease Lemon's interest? John frowned and turned away from her.

He found he wanted to look at her, so he went to the far end of the fireplace and lay his arm along the mantel. There he was in the shadows and she couldn't see him, except as a white shirtfront.

She knew she had his attention. She moved as a woman does when she is being observed by an attractive man. She lifted her chin, turned her head and licked her lips. She was busily indifferent to him.

She finger combed her hair, sliding her fingers into the mass and lifting it back.

He was mesmerized.

She lifted her arms and stretched.

He sucked in a breath.

She leaned over and threw a stick onto the fire.

He was riveted.

She asked casually, "How did such a man get the name of John Brown?"

His brain had a little trouble jump-starting his tongue. He blurted, "My adoptive father is named Brown. Salty Brown."

"Salty?"

"He was a sailor. A twenty-year man."

"So you're John Brown." She looked at the white shirtfront, knowing his head was above that because she occasionally saw a glint of light reflected in his eyes. She sang sadly, "John Brown's body lies a-moldering in his grave—"

"So you're a singing drunk."

"I am not drunk. I have been very careful how much I've had."

"That bottle is almost empty."

"It was that way when I picked it up."

"Then you're not feeling soft and pliant?"

"Not at all. I'm a little restless." She looked up at him and saw his white teeth above his white shirt-front. "In the shadows, that way, you look like a bodiless head."

"I feel that way." He coughed a couple of times.

Apparently, he raised a fist to cover his cough because his shirtfront disappeared and so did his teeth.

His eyes were apparently closed, because there was no light-catching glint from them.

"You've vanished."

"I'm a vampire," he admitted with a nicely rueful tone. "Do you hear the flapping of my bat wings?"

"Don't bite my neck."

"I'm not especially hooked on just necks. I can bite anywhere."

She sighed gustily. "One of those."

"That kind of reply makes me very curious as to the men you know."

"I've known very few, and they were all just as nice as they could be. But women do mention odd things now and again. That's why women get together. They spread the word."

"And in all that information, you never heard anything about Lemon?"

"Oh, yes."

Gravely serious, he said, "Oh."

"That's why I refused to come here until you said you'd be here."

"Me?" That annoyed him.

"Yes. You have a very nice reputation among the women who know you."

Somehow that offended him. He took a couple of steps, and his mouth worked as he tried to give a wicked man's laughing response, but he didn't know one. What would Lemon say to that? He'd say...he'd say... "Well, that's nice to hear!"

"You're surprised you have a good reputation?"

"Startled."

With a touch of caution, she asked, "Why are you startled?"

And his clever tongue told the exact truth. "I'm surprised any woman would discuss me in any circumstances."

"Why?"

He put out a hand, palm up, and said flatly, "There's nothing to discuss."

"Someone said there was a woman—" She stopped.

He encouraged her reply. "So?"

"One you cared about."

"And..."

"Her name was Priscilla."

He corrected, "Lucilla."

"So you still remember her name?"

"I went with her for some time."

"You never married."

There was some bitterness evident. Even he heard it as he replied, "No. She declined."

"Why?"

With a touch of irritation, he said honestly, "I'm really quite dull."

She smiled with just the softening of her face. "And the dullness attracted the space alien, because he knew you wouldn't give him any trouble?"

With the wording of her question, he realized she'd declined to accept that he was dull. He looked at her, sitting there in that nothing dress and looking like an angel watching him, and he responded with, "Probably."

She put back her head and laughed.

In all of his life, he had never felt so flattered. He took another step or two and said, "Most humans decline to admit to meeting an alien. They think people will look at them with more care."

"I look on most men with care," she told him aloofly. "Men are another race altogether."

"No, you have that wrong. If you've read your Bible, you know that men were here first."

"How nice for you."

"We went wild. We had to have a sobering influence. Something to cope with and something to work for. A challenge. A purpose."

"How boring."

"I'd think you'd be flattered. We treasure women for that reason. You make our lives worthwhile."

"A man, dear alien, sets his wife up in an endlessly dirt-accumulating house, while he goes adventuring. He returns periodically and generously gives her another child. Then she gets her own car so he doesn't have to ferry the kids around, do the shopping or run the endless errands necessary. And most of the time she, additionally, has to work at a job."

"But he comes home and checks up on her now and then."

"Probably only to give her another child."

"I thought there was an effort for population zero."

"Not too many are trying for that. Hardly anyone in the rest of the world is interested. I saw an environmental cartoon of people like a smothering swarm of bees clinging on the globe and some were being crowded off to fall into space."

"So you don't want any children?"

She replied soberly, "The allotted two and one-third."

He frowned in thought. "How do you have a third of a child?"

"I'm not sure. Have you recovered from what's-her-name?"

"Lucilla," he supplied kindly. And he looked at Margot for solemn seconds. "I do believe I'll survive." To his surprise, the words were easily said.

"Good." She shifted as if to dismiss a tasteless subject and discard it altogether. But then she added, "Women also talk about other women. Priscilla's name has been mentioned a time or two."

"Lucilla." He put in gently.

"I know." She licked her lips and gave him an innocent, big-eyed look. "The women have known her—forever." She did minutely stress that last word. Then, having underlined the fact that Lucilla was probably at least somewhat older than John, Margot had to add, "Her birth certificate says...Priscilla, and her hair roots are a mousy brown."

He laughed.

Although she appeared disdainful, she was inordinately pleased to hear his nice laugh. "They said she dumped you because she thought if she was free of you she'd get a shot at Lemon, but she underestimated Lemon's loyalty to you."

"Yeah?"

"Lemon wouldn't touch her with a ten-foot pole."

And that did surprise John. "How do you know that?"

"Some of the women witnessed her...bold... attempts."

"Those women have busy mouths."

"I just thought you ought to know what is being said."

"You gossip."

"No." She shook her head. "No, no, no. Don't misunderstand. I listen."

"So you listen to gossip?"

"I listen to—and see—a lot of things. Like tone of voice, looks exchanged, things said. Contradictions. All of those things give you ideas about people. Then you can test them."

"Are you testing me?"

"I came here to meet you."

"Well, that's certainly clear enough. I thought you came here, wearing Lemon's gift—" he really bore down on that "—in order to have a chance at him."

She sighed and flopped back with her arms out and her hands upon the sofa pillows on either side of her. "Men can be so insufferably stupid."

"And women are so easily read? Come on, Margot, men are simple creatures. God made you all the way you are so that we have to constantly puzzle you out. That way we can't possibly get bored."

She was amazed. "You can't be implying that Priscilla was fascinating!"

He smoothed the thick hair on the top of his head and licked at his smile. "She was very—interesting."

"But what did you do the other ninety-eight hours out of a hundred?" However, Margot couldn't leave it at that, so she blurted, "I'd bet she found those other two hours really yucky."

He laughed out loud. He put back his head and really laughed. He looked at her. He tried to stop. He looked away, rubbed his nose and took carefully casual paces but he could not, not laugh.

She tilted her head around and lifted her eyebrows and was patient.

He said with some kind humor, "I took you for a really wild and woolly party girl."

"You weren't paying attention."

"So, you're not? What are you doing in that dress?"

"I thought it might catch your eye."

"You've caught it. But you don't act according to what that dress implies."

"How do you mean?"

The door rattled and someone knocked, but with the silence within the room, they laughed and went on their way.

John paid no attention. He was concentrated on Margot. He explained, "You're prickly and snippy and difficult."

"Good grief! What did you think I'd be?"

"Mmm...more pliant?"

She bobbed a series of nods. "Down on the floor, spread-eagled," she guessed.

"Why, you *did* know! Exactly."

"No."

"Why not?" His reaction was somewhere between real surprise and pretend indignation. "You admit to being here to meet me. What better way to get acquainted?"

"Has this approach ever been successful?"

"Not yet."

And she laughed, her eyes sparkled and she looked at him with such amusement.

He thought she was charming. He grinned back at her and asked, "A little more wine? It's time for you to wet your tongue with the wine."

"Maybe you're more observant than I thought."

"You did actually have one sip. You burped and sneezed."

"So you really were here first."

"How else could I have gotten in?"

"From what I've heard, you can do anything."

He considered her soberly, with curiosity, but he didn't ask.

She expanded the premise. "You jumped the fence with Lemon's pinto."

"That's wonderful. He wanted to jump it, I didn't, and he won."

"See? That's what everyone says about you. Whatever feat you accomplish, you say it was an accident."

"It was! That damned horse is no good."

"Lemon loves him, and the horse will now jump the fence for Lemon. You taught the pinto to do that."

"He's a stupid horse, but he has the right instincts. The mares are always on the other side of fences... ergo, he jumps fences." He gave her a gradually increasingly lazy look. "I, too, jump fences."

"That doesn't surprise me. How many have you jumped?"

"Like the pinto, I'm still learning to just clear the fence without vital injuries." He looked so smoky eyed and amused.

She scoffed and said, "Sure."

"We could test it. There's a fence just out the side door. We could get you over on the other side, and I'd show you how I get over the fence."

"How do you do it, with a hand on top and legs swung over?"

He shook his head.

"Run and jump?"

"No."

She opened out her hands. "How?"

"I have a handy ladder."

She groaned and put her hand to her face as she laughed.

"I can also reach second-story windows," he offered. "It's an extension ladder."

"I have no intention of sleeping with you."

"You're on the third floor?" He was appalled.

"No."

He gestured. "Things happen. Events occur. Volcanoes erupt. There are cosmic collisions. Surprises can surprise us all."

She gave a tolerant sigh and said, "Nope."

"It's fated."

"Not yet."

"When?"

"Are you a sex fiend?"

"Just tonight. I've wanted you since I saw you wiggling around on the dance floor and carrying on like that wild and woolly woman you appear to be."

"I didn't mean to do anything but to make you look at me."

"Well, you made every male here look at you in the same way I did."

"Don't be silly."

"How could you come here, wearing Lemon's dress and claim you wanted to meet me? How can a man get friendly with a woman when his friend bought her a skimpy, wicked dress?"

"My being in Lemon's dress hasn't slowed you down at all. In turn, Lemon would have nothing to do with Priscilla. Who is a friend?"

"You want me to back off?"

She looked at him soberly. "No."

He smiled. "When are you going to sleep with me?"

"Oh, I could do that tonight. It's just that I simply will not make love with you."

"Now how could you possibly sleep in the same bed with me and not make love?"

She gestured with rather annoyed openness and said the obvious, "By not doing it!"

He sat on the couch and put his head in his hands. "You strain a man."

She was indignant. "I haven't touched you!"

"You wore that damned dress."

"There is more material in this dress than there is in ten postage-stamp swimsuits. Maybe twenty!"

He lifted his head and frowned at her. "Do you wear a swimsuit like that?"

"No."

"Well, I guess that's something to be thankful for. How many men have you slept with?"

"None."

He was shocked. "Never?"

She was prickly. "Never. What's the big deal about that?"

"You never have and you'd wear THAT DRESS?"

She jumped up and leaned over, causing him to gasp, but she was yelling, "What is it about this DRESS? You've talked about nothing else since I found you over there by the window, being an alien!" There was some censoring in the sound of her strident voice.

"It was the dress. It sent me into orbit."

She took hold of the hem and said in a very hostile way, "I'll take it off and just wear the slip!"

In astonishment, he exclaimed, "You have on a slip?"

"Good gravy, John, you really are from outer space. Women do wear slips. What kind of woman have you—well, I can see your problem."

She let go of the hem in an irritated manner and walked over to the table to wet her tongue with wine.

So he didn't have a heart attack after all.

During the following very pregnant pause, someone knocked on the door and called, "Food."

Margot went over and unlocked the door as John's heart lost all heart. She was leaving.

She opened the door only a sliver and asked, "For whom?"

"Who all's in there?" It was one of the serving people hired by the caterer.

"A cart?"

"Yeah. Want it?"

"Just push it in. We'll serve ourselves."

"It's almost ten, and we'll be around all night. Punch four on the phone if you need anything. Happy New Year."

"Thank you. Happy New Year."

"And to everyone else in there."

John said in seven different male voices, "Happy New Year."

Margot maneuvered the cart into the room in a blocking way and said, "It looks marvelous. Good night."

The waiter warned, "Plug in the hot plate."

She replied, "I shall."

She closed and locked the door again. That gave John great hope. Any man who can get a woman into a locked room with food available doesn't have to give up hope yet.

She questioned, "All those voices? How'd you do that? You've ruined my reputation. What will they think in the kitchen?"

"They wouldn't be at all surprised. Not with you wearing that dress."

"That again!" She gave him a quelling glance, then busied herself with the food.

John got up, went over to observe and chose what he wanted to eat. He asked, "How well do you know Lemon?"

"We've known each other for a while. He used to date one of my sisters."

"How old are you?"

"My goodness to gracious, you are subtle."

He looked at her closely, leaning over and narrowing his eyes. "Over eighteen?"

She replied, "I'm twenty-six."

He didn't believe her.

She raised her hand and put the other on her heart. "On my honor."

"And you've never..."

"Never."

He wasn't sure he believed her. Either the claimed age was wrong and she was younger or she wasn't truthful. What woman could hold out that long?

"Did you miss with Lemon and decide on me?"

"No, he's never interested me. My sister only dated him for a while. They're still good friends. They just didn't suit each other."

"I don't mind if you tried for Lemon. He's an unusual man and very attractive to women. He could have about any woman he wanted, even if he didn't have the means he has. I really wouldn't mind—if you were over him by now, you understand—I just have to see from where I have to start...with you."

"I'm not attracted to him."

He couldn't swallow that. He scoffed and laughed at her humor for saying such a thing.

She shrugged. "He isn't attracted to me, either. We're casual friends."

He watched her as if she would betray herself in a lie. Then he asked quickly, "What was Lemon saying to you—all that time on your porch?"

"He was telling me what a sterling character you are."

"You're teasing."

"Honest!" She spread some stuff on a cracker and handed him one. "Try this."

He was cautious. He took it gingerly and tasted it carefully. It was excellent. He began to look through the foods and found a supply of bottles on the shelf at the bottom of the cart. They had expected to serve more than two people from that cart.

He read the bottle labels and nodded. He said, "No Alle."

"Shucks." Her tone was unfeeling.

He told her, "You're a strange woman."

She gave him a superior glance and commented, "I've never harbored an alien."

Three

———

John put his small brandy glass aside. He needed to be careful. He needed his wits about him. Then he just looked at Margot. In all of his life, he hadn't met anyone who came close to her who was of his age.

There had been Felicia, his stepmother, whom he'd always considered so unique that she was incomparable.

But now there was a chance that he'd found a woman who could compare. She hadn't Felicia's drama. She didn't use her voice as Felicia played with hers so casually. But Margot was more than any woman he'd yet known. She might be precious.

Even above the distant sound of revelry from the ballroom at the other end of the house, there was the sound of the wind rising. John was aware of it subconsciously as he watched the fascinating woman who was Margot Pulver.

She was busily preparing, combining, selecting and offering him tastes and samplings. It annoyed him that she was even slightly distracted from him. Then he realized that she was garnering the goodies for him.

She handed him the plate, utensils and a napkin. She lifted interested brows and asked, "Wine?"

"There's a good white here that ought to be okay with this selection of foods."

"You sound as if you're an expert on wines."

"It goes with the territory."

"What—territory?"

"Lemon entertains a lot. He's taught me wines. He's remarkably knowledgeable—on many things."

"People," she supplied. "He sure knows people."

"I think that talent's inborn."

"So do you know people." She gave him that compliment quite casually. "You're better at it than he. You can size up a man in just one meeting and you're right."

"How did you decide that?"

"My front-porch visit with Lemon."

And since he'd wondered about it, this was his chance to ask her, "Why didn't you ask him into the house?"

"I was alone. I never have a man inside when there's no one else around."

"Why not?" He was somewhat male-indignant. "Not all men are lecherous."

"No, but why struggle with the ones who are?"

"You're locked in here, alone with me."

"Yeah." She smiled at him, very amused.

"How do you know that I wouldn't?"

"I can scream like a calliope on a high note."

"Wow!"

She preened.

"Then you could have screamed when Lemon was there."

"A calliope high note is hard on the throat." She very kindly shared that information. "There was no need for him to be inside, so I didn't let him in."

"What if it'd been blowing a blue norther?"

"He could have come back, and we do have a phone."

"So you're careful." He considered her. "But you've locked that door twice now, with me in here with you. The second time was deliberate. How come?"

"I'm compromising you."

"Bull."

"I honestly don't want anyone interrupting. I want to know you."

"Uhh..." He drew that out as he considered. He walked a couple of steps contemplating the Oriental rug under his feet. Then he said in a musing way, "You wanted to meet me, and now you want to know me. Scars and moles next?" He lifted his glass for a blasé sip of wine, as any man in control would do.

But she said an airy, "Not yet."

He choked and coughed, so she pounded on his back and told him to raise his left arm as high as he could. He coughed and did that. It worked.

He told her with some irritation, "If you're going to surprise me with your sassy answers, warn me."

"Yes, sir."

"Good attitude."

"I'm not sure if this is sassy, but if we get past this initial interview, and you are still acceptable, we might well get to the mole-and-scar segment."

"I think I'll sit down."

"Too much wine?"

"I think it's the dress. It over-mans me."

"Over...mans?" She frowned. Then she began to smile. "Oh."

"You just don't flirt along the accepted lines. I don't know which side is up. But—"

She giggled.

He chided, "Stop that."

"I was just appreciating your humor."

"You're not supposed to catch on that quick."

"—ly."

"Hmm?"

"Quickly."

"Yeah." He considered her somewhat sourly. "How many of your old boyfriends are in mental institutions, sitting in corners and mumbling: '...and THEN she said...'?"

"None. I've never wanted to be completely honest with any other man."

"I'm not sure that's good."

"Since there's a cloth on the tea cart, why don't we just raise the drop leaves and use it for a table?"

"Okay." He got up and went for chairs. They each weighed a ton. He wrestled them into place. "Let me see you try to knock one of those over."

"Why?"

"They are so solid, you couldn't possibly lift one."

"That's why I raised the cart leaves. I knew you could handle those chairs."

"I think I sprung something vital. I can't be sure. Perhaps you would..."

She was searching her plate for a bite and didn't even bother to look up. "That's about the clumsiest ploy I've ever heard."

"Who else tried to get you to examine them?"

"I believe the first one was named Joe D. Or was it Barney? I'm not sure."

"When was that?"

"I must have been about—umm—five. Frances told me to ignore them."

"Anyone lately?"

"Some guy in a library who—"

"You think I was trying to—" He tightened his lips. "Well, I am surprised you'd think that of me. Not after you've had such sterling reports on me."

She explained with courtesy, "Men don't always act the same way to other men or women as they might behave alone with one woman."

"You think I'm out of line?"

She grinned as she said sassily, "Honey, you'll still be throwing lines when you're a hundred-twenty, in a wheelchair in a nursing home."

He looked blandly interested. "A home for nursing mothers?"

"See?"

"Why aren't you offended by me?"

"You're testing me because Priscilla hurt your ego."

"Lucilla."

"Whatever. How could your eye have been caught by that type of woman? I have puzzled on that for some time."

"When was that?"

"I saw you last year at Lemon's party."

"In San Antone?"

"Yep."

"You were there?"

"If I saw you there, I had to have been there."

"I can't believe I missed seeing you."

"You weren't looking. And when you were looking around, you were looking for that one woman."

"I could have known you for a whole year by now."

"No, it was important for you to know Priscilla before you could appreciate me."

He grinned and his eyes danced with lights as he watched her and slowly shook his head in a chiding way.

"Some men are like that." She continued her lecture as she pulled bits of meat from the drumstick in her hand and put them into her mouth to chew. She licked her fingers very casually, as if all people did that when they were eating, and she did it elegantly as she said in a lifted-eyebrow voice, "I once saw two dogs in our side yard. I thought one had been hit by a car. It was lying on its stomach and panting. It was a long-haired part husky and its coat was very like Priscilla's hair...ends."

"Okay, it hadn't been hit by a car. And?"

"There was a big dog guarding the fluff. He was shorthaired, big-boned and silent, but very alert. Very quiet. I was touched when the big dog went over and licked the smaller dog's nose. I was about to quit watching and go call the humane society when the fluff got up."

"She was all right?"

"She limped. She crossed the street with the big dog close by. They went across the street by a house. I went out to see which way they were going when two other dogs met them. The bitch was in heat."

She didn't look at John. She busily, indifferently sought through the goodies on her plate to choose another bite and lifted it to taste it. It was then that she allowed her gaze to rest on her companion.

"You think Priscilla is the bitch."

Margot was astonished by that conclusion, but she managed to keep a sober face and struggled not to mention his recognizing Priscilla. She lost the struggle. "How did you know? I know. It was the hair color! The dog's coloring was all the way—no roots showing. Of course, it could have been a fresh rinse."

He shook his head, chiding her. "You are really awful! Do you realize that? Here I came into this room and closed the doors to grieve, because after midnight I'll be in a year that I wasn't with Pri—LU-cilla."

"How wonderfully romantic!" She clasped her hands against her chest. Then she opened her fingers and put her hands out discreetly. "What a klutz she was to spurn you. I can't believe she'd be that dumb." She gestured in little hand turnings. She shook her head in amazed incomprehension. "And her roots are *mouse brown*—not even *blond!* No excuse." She lifted one hand out by her shoulder. She went on emphatically, "None at all! You made a lucky escape."

She dismissed even considering something so foolish. She licked her lips busily in tiny, little movements, and looked at her plate, choosing, discarding, as she moved her body a trifle. Her back was straight and her whole attention was on the food. But then she peeked up at him to find him mesmerized, and she smiled with such wicked humor that he laughed.

She went back to eating. And he sat back in his chair and watched her. He said, "If you aren't actually considering me, if you are just testing your skills on me, you would be kind to back off from me." Before she could reply, he added, "After midnight."

She tilted her head back and looked at him down her nose. "After midnight?"

"I want a kiss from you."

"Okay. One."

"Or two or so."

She was back to selections and didn't look at him. She said, "We'll try one."

"With an option."

"I'll reread the contract. I don't recall any options."

Exasperated, he complained, "I don't know why we ever let women go to school."

"They don't now in Iran. And there are other places where men stop women from learning."

"I really didn't mean for you to get out your soapbox."

Her look was sober. "It's a serious subject."

"I'll allow that it is. How's that?"

"Such a concession!"

He said thoughtfully, "I believe you'd be a handful. I'd better go a little slower and see about you. You could scare a man pretty bad."

She looked at him and smiled slightly with that same humor.

And he smiled a little as he nodded with his thought, "But you might be worth the tangle."

"Tangle?"

"As opposed to smooth."

She considered him. "You prefer your life simple?"

"It sure would help."

"I prefer a man who works with a woman to a man who dictates or one who rules or somebody who follows and endures."

"I wonder how we'd be in a double hitch. You'd want to leave the track and pick the bluebonnets."

"Perhaps. It would depend on why we were pulling whatever to where."

"Yes. I can see that."

"Have you tried these?" She put two rice crackers with shrimp and some sauce with a curl of parsley on his plate. Then she watched with interest in his reaction as he lifted one to his mouth and ate it thoughtfully. He nodded, "Good."

"Try this." She put another out between her thumb and two fingers and lay it on his hand. It was caviar with a slice of hard-boiled egg and a sprig of watercress.

He lifted his head a little and put it into his mouth to taste it. He nodded as he chewed then swallowed.

She waited until he was finished. Then she suggested, "Have a little wine to freshen your palate. Then try this." It was ground meat, egg, relish, peas, onion and seasonings. It was outrageously delicious.

He said, "Spam."

"How'd you know?"

"You had me freshen my palate, and it just... knew."

"How vulgar of you."

She made him smile.

She looked at the tiny-nothing watch that circled her wrist. "It's after eleven. Would you like some pensive time to long for old what's-her-face?"

He was briefly surprised that she would remember that. Quite honestly, he replied, "I don't believe so."

"If we should last through this initial interview and become serious, twenty years from now I don't want you mentioning that I interrupted your nostalgic immersion in melancholy, for Priscilla of the drab hair roots."

"Priscilla...who?"

She lifted her eyebrows and bowed her head once. "We may make it."

"Do I have to wait for midnight to test your manner of kissing?"

She looked at him as if surprised that he'd inquired. "Of course."

"What a stickler!"

Rather prissily, she declared, "Anticipation is half the fun."

Just that quick, he promised, "Wait'll you try the other half."

She burst out laughing. She did try to control it, but she went right back to laughter and her eyes brimmed with her humor as she sneaked peeks at him.

He'd been carried along and his own eyes were filled with laughter...and his delight in her.

They discussed each of the other choices in nibbles and debated which was more delicious. They agreed most of the time. She accused him of disagreeing just to show that he wasn't easily led. He had the audacity to agree to that. And she laughed.

With midnight nearing, and the wind sounding serious, they finished their cheesecake and had a bit more wine.

She looked again at her tiny watch and said, "I must freshen up. Can you stay and protect this haven from invaders until I get back?"

"I'll do it."

"Excellent." She rose from her chair, and he reached to help her with it as he, too, rose.

He lifted the chair aside.

She noted that, watching with some patience. "You can lift that chair."

"Damn, now you won't help me."

"Help you ... what?"

"Hold the door. Lift the fig leaf, cope with life's little annoyances."

"I'll see."

"There's hope!"

She had moved to the door but stopped and said, "Don't push it."

He came and unlocked the door for her. Then he looked at her, his lashes shading his eyes. His smile was just about as wicked as such a smile can manage.

"What are you thinking?"

"I thought I might go along and guard the door but if I did we wouldn't have this room to ourselves. Someone may come along and want to share."

"I'll be careful."

"So will I, but don't attract any man loose and looking."

"I'd never do that."

"Wait. I'll check to see if the coast is clear ... and even the hall."

She took a deep, patient breath. He watched that, instead. Then he looked at the ceiling, and finally he opened the door and looked down the hall. He said in a whisper, "It's clear. Be quick."

So when she came back, he said, "I must comb my eyebrows, it's your turn to guard our sanctuary."

"Wait. Two salacious women are coming along, searching for any male."

"Oh." He moved as if to open the door and was delighted when she gasped and put out her hand.

He stood still, grinning and delighted.

"You're a fraud."

"Only testing."

She looked at him and understood he was referring to her statement that she listened and judged and tested people.

She checked the hall, and it was briefly clear.

She motioned, and he took the door to open it wider. "Don't let anyone in."

She whispered, "I won't."

With them so quiet, they could hear the fury of the building storm.

He slid out of the room and disappeared. She locked the door and waited. He came back and tapped. "It's I, the alien."

"Oh." She opened the door, and it was he.

He said, "How'd you know which alien?"

"I've only known one."

"I forgot to choose a password and figured you might recognize that."

He locked the door. She stood and soberly watched. That was the third time she'd been locked inside the room with him. She looked at him, and he was intensely interested, watching her.

He said, "It'll soon be midnight."

"A new year. Another year."

"A fresh year." He said that with some satisfaction as he lifted his head and looked around the room. His gaze stopped on Adam.

He turned his head to observe his companion. She was considering him. He asked, "What are you thinking?"

"I've never kissed a beard before."

"Well, come to think of it, neither have I."

She put up her hand. "Let me feel."

He backed a step and asked in shock, "Feel? What?" He crossed his hands in front of his body.

She looked at the ceiling and complained, "I get locked in a room with a comedian. I want to feel your beard. If it's rough, I'll let you out before midnight— we have three minutes and you can hunt down some woman who likes prickly beards."

"Feel." He was serious as he leaned his face toward her. "If you don't like it, I'll shave it off."

She was close in order to feel his beard. Her arms were up. Her attention was on his beard. "It's nice! It's soft. I like i—"

And he kissed her. He took her body against his and his arms held her to him as he really kissed her.

After a time, panting, he lifted his head and stared at her with hot eyes.

She said, "Wow. Oh, my. My goodness. That was... really nice. I had no idea." She swallowed noisily and her breaths were a little fast. She said, "Maybe you ought to let me go."

The winds were stronger and rattling loose shutters. The party sounds were picking up. There was a mob counting down from ten. They could hear all that in the silence of the locked library.

"Five... four..."

Their gazes met very seriously. Their anticipation made their hearts beat more quickly. She was plastered against his body, and he could feel the softness of her squashed against him. He shivered. She had to breathe through her mouth. Her lips were red from his first kiss. He would kiss her again. She'd limited him to one. She wouldn't mention that now.

"Two...ONE! Happy New Year!"

There were the distant horns and the dragging music of "Auld Lang Syne" became audible with dragging voices drowning out the sounds of the wind.

John continued to hold her that close, and he watched her face. He was very serious. He slowly pulled her impossibly closer as he lowered his mouth to hers, his lips claiming and melding with hers, and it was exactly the same chaos rioting through her body. It was shocking!

For a woman who had never before experienced intense sexual hunger, it was amazing. She'd been attracted to men, and being hugged and kissed had been pleasant. But this was different. This was need! This temptation was for flinging-her-hat-over-the-windmill type of abandon.

It scared her even as it thrilled her. She was shocked by her hips, which curled her against him. And she acknowledged what was poking her in the stomach. He was aroused.

It was a little crass of him to be so obvious, so quick.

He lifted his mouth slowly from hers and there were tiny sounds of the parting. She noticed that her body stretched up along him a little. Her mouth was following his, not wanting the kiss to end. She thought in appalled shock, Why, Margot Pulver! Shame on you.

He groaned in deep misery. He put his head down alongside hers and just squeezed her to him. And she could feel his hands tremble. She'd done that to him? This was what her mother had warned her about. This was what other women referred to and rolled their eyes and sighed about. This was what she wasn't supposed to let happen. And in her twenty-six years, it hadn't. Now what was she supposed to do?

And she remembered the musical *Oklahoma* and the woman who just couldn't say no. Could *she* be that spineless?

Surely not.

Four

John slowly lifted his head enough so that his stunned eyes could see Margot's face.

She could feel his right hand on her back. The heel of his hand was at one side of her back, his fingers were wrapped around to the other side over her hip-bone. His thumb was up between her shoulder blades and his littlest finger was at the top of her buttocks. His fingers had octopus suction cups— It was all impossible.

John cleared his throat twice and his eyes were intense. He said in a husky voice, "We'd better go join the others."

Margot looked blank. Couldn't the others join themselves? She blinked a time or two and concentrated seriously. He was speaking of getting out of that isolated, locked library and being with others until they could calm down. How smart he was. He knew he was in danger from her, and he'd solved the problem like a gentleman.

He asked, "Are you okay?"

She wobbled her head as she released her hold on him.

He allowed her escape as he said, "You're a danger to mankind."

She just wobbled her head again. Then she tried to walk. How did one do that again? Uh, one foot at a time and shift balance. That shifting balance was tricky.

John watched her effort as he smoothed his hair and then his beard, then he rubbed his stomach and practiced breathing. He wasn't concerned about walking in a normal way, he just managed somehow to get to the library door.

He slowly, carefully unlocked the door; then he straightened and just stared at her. She was still concentrating on walking.

He opened the door hesitantly, reluctant to give up their sanctuary. She didn't say anything. She was still determined to walk normally, and she managed to get to the door. Then she glanced up at him.

It was such a...stunned look. Her eyes were three inches tall and two and a half inches wide. She looked at him, but it wasn't in revulsion. She'd really been surprised by his kiss. She was twenty-six years old and had never been surprised by a kiss? He began to smile a little.

She continued to study him from the safety of that opened doorway. She whispered, "Wow." It was a tiny, breathless sound. She was very serious.

He gasped in shock. His shiver was a sexual one as his blood rushed in avid concentration.

Margot turned slowly away. She managed to get out of the doorway and into the hall. It took him a minute to gear up and follow. Fortunately, it was some distance across the house to the ballroom. They moved slowly, not speaking. She was still struggling to get control of her body.

So was he, struggling with his own body. He was restless and his hand moved to his face or beard or hair or stomach and his other hand touched her. He put his hand to her back at her waist, supposedly to aid in her struggle to walk, but it was really just to touch her.

They'd known each other mere hours. How could it be? How could such a hot attraction occur in such a relatively short time? He'd seen her twice. Once as she'd talked to another man on her porch, and again for just over three hours of intense concentration in a locked library. Incredible.

As they walked toward the ballroom, the big house shivered in the onslaught of the winds. Hearing it was about the only thing that distracted John from Margot. He was peripherally aware of something outside of his fascination for her.

Men are generally that way. Their attention can be riveted, but their sense of place would still be working. John knew there was a storm building. He knew that even before he saw Clint, Lemon's cattleman.

Clint was standing in the main hall that led to the entrance. He was in rough clothes, his sheepskin-lined coat was open because of the heat in the house. The coat was the long kind with a slit up the back so that a horse-riding man had the coattails to cover his thighs. He had on a Stetson with the cord up to his chin to hold it on, and under the hat was a woolen kerchief tied around his head and ears.

Clint heard a woman's high heels on the bare floor between the rugs, and as they approached Clint turned slowly to see the woman. He didn't see John right away. He saw Margot in that dress.

John watched Clint as they walked toward the entrance hall, and Clint finally looked to see the man with whom the woman was walking. He glanced a dismissive flick at John, but then Clint's eyes came back and he regarded John soberly before he smiled just a bit.

John asked, "Is it bad?"

Clint removed his hat in courtesy to Margot as he replied to John, "Blue."

That was clear enough. A blue norther. The worst kind. "Need help?"

Clint shook his head. "Just reporting."

"That damned pinto in?"

Clint grinned. Their opinions of the pinto paralleled. "Yeah. First."

"So you didn't favor trying to convince the pinto to go to the barn during the storm?" They both knew John said all that for Margot's information. John smiled a tad.

Clint's eye crinkles deepened. "I'd know to come straight to you—since you taught him to jump fences."

"You're all heart."

And Margot's kiss-softened puffed lips smiled a little. The storm had made no impression in her fogged mind, but she did remember John complaining about Lemon's pinto.

Clint couldn't resist a comment on John's companion. Mostly because John had neglected to introduce him to the dazed woman, Clint said to John. "Keep her inside, in that dress."

John knew Clint meant to call his attention to the fact that Clint had noted the dress on her, but Margot assumed the man speaking meant it would be too cold outside without a coat. Men and women hear things differently. Clint smiled.

John said, "I'll attend to her."

Clint replied, "I just bet you'll try."

And John said, "Careful."

Margot said, "—ly."

So John corrected, "Speak carefully." His glance warned Clint to be quiet.

Clint said to Margot, "He has rough edges."

Margot inquired soberly, "Where?"

But Clint laughed.

Margot frowned a little, thinking over the conversation, and didn't see the humor. She glanced at John, who had his stern regard on Clint.

John said, "Watch out for yourself."

That could mean anything. Margot assumed that John was concerned for this man to be out in the storm, but Clint knew John was warning him to behave in front of the woman. Clint said to her, "I'm Clint Terrell."

Margot responded, "How do you do?"

John tugged at Margot's arm.

Clint replied to Margot, "I'll find out."

As John tugged her away from Clint, Margot asked, "What does he need to find out?"

"Nothing."

From behind them, Clint laughed in his throat the woman-luring way men have which is so wicked. Margot might have noticed the laugh if it hadn't been for the double-whammy killer kiss she'd gotten from John just before then. John's kiss had been a temporary immunizing factor. A few more of that kind, and Margot might not ever look at another man. Those double-whammy ones were fatal to a roving eye.

Just about all the guests were in the ballroom. There was confetti everywhere, in streamers or with loose bits in hair, some caught in clothes creases and some lay in swirls on the floor.

Everyone was wearing one of the paper hats, and a good many had horns, which were being blown. The horn-din, party-pitched talking and laughing made for bedlam.

Since John and Margot were the only hatless ones in the room, some man said in an aside to John, "Not around for the hats?"

"When they passed them out, they missed us."

The man laughed and pointed. "Over there."

But Lemon came along with party hats. He had picked up a bunch, so it appeared he was seeing to it no one was hatless, not that he was supplying them particularly to John and Margot.

John said to Lemon, "I didn't know the fig leaf on Adam was movable."

"So you peeked?" Lemon was exquisitely amused.

"Margot did."

Lemon chided her, "Shame on you."

"What's under it?" John asked.

"Didn't you look?"

"No, I was distracted."

"So it was you two locked in the library?"

Margot was astonished, but she was recovering because she immediately asked John, "Was the door locked?"

He replied easily, "It was just stuck."

And Lemon laughed.

For some distraction, John asked, "Did you see Clint?"

"No. Is he here?" Lemon stretched up and looked around as he called out in the noisy crowd, "Men, guard your women. Clint Terrell, the terror, is here!"

To Lemon, John supplied the information, "He's out in the center hall."

"Charlie must be looking for me. I'll go find Clint. Tell Charlie you found me. Okay?"

"Sure."

John took Margot in tow and looked for Charlie. He was behind the bar looking at bottle labels. John scolded, "Now how did you think you were going to find Lemon back there?"

Unperturbed, Charlie didn't even look up. Still judging the labels, he replied, "We got a blue norther on us, and we could be holed up for a couple of very boring days...and nights. There's no hurry."

"I found Lemon and sent him to Clint."

Mildly, still looking at the labels, Charlie chided, "That was interfering with my duties."

"Clint would've gotten bored waiting out there in the hall."

"I'm working under his orders." Charlie glanced up, saw Margot and looked at that dress. "Well, hello there, honey. You play poker?"

She shook her head minutely as John said, "No." Then he took off his tux jacket and put it on Margot. It was as long as the dress, and she appeared to be wearing only the tux jacket. Well, win some, lose some. He left it on her. No one could see through the jacket.

Lemon came back into the ballroom with Clint, and they came over to the bar. Clint was looking around and nodding to specific women. His smile was a predator's smile. They came to the bar, and Clint said to Margot, "I'd recognize those legs anywhere. What happened to that sinful dress?"

"Sinful?"

Clint said, "Yeah," drawing out the word salaciously as his eye crinkles deepened.

She said, "You're going to roast in that coat in here."

Clint ignored that to ask, "How come you're wearing John's tux jacket?"

"I don't know. Charlie asked if I played poker and all of a sudden I was in John's jacket." She looked innocent.

Clint asked, "Do you?"

"I hesitate to ask. Do I what?"

John supplied the reply, "No."

Clint asked John, "Do I know you?"

And Margot explained, "He's an alien."

Clint gasped in exaggerated delight and exclaimed, "I'm an alien, too!"

Margot scoffed, "What border did you cross?"

And Clint watched her in such a smoky way. "Any you'd put up."

John said seriously, "That's enough, Clint."

"You gotta realize Charlie and I've got to go out in this cold, mean weather? You have to know we'll be holed up together for a couple of days, more than likely? And he's already smelling ripe. Now what do you suppose I'll have to think on during all that time?"

"Not her."

Clint looked so innocent. He opened out both hands to show he was. He said, "Now would I do a thing like that? I was talking about getting a couple of bottles to salute the New Year!"

Lemon said, "No. You'd both pass out, and we'd dig your frozen bodies out in a couple of days."

"Well," Clint pretended concern. "How about this one coming along and keeping us interested and awake?" He paused while that soaked in; then he explained innocently, "We could play cards."

She asked, "Why would you be out in this weather, anyway?"

"We won't be far. We'll be out, nearby, so as we can keep the herds from drifting. Drifting cattle can fall into ravines, canyons, rivers, all that fun stuff."

Lemon said, "No booze."

Charlie explained in a very careful way, "We're putting these two bottles aside to have when the weather clears. We agreed not to come to the party, but it's only fair that we get some of the booze."

"I've already put yours aside."

Charlie asked, "What" in a statement, encouraging a reply.

"Your regular rotgut."

Charlie chided, "Our taste buds is getting more sophisticated."

Clint corrected, "Our palates, they are a-changing." He told Charlie in an aside, "You gotta talk so's he'll know what you mean."

Margot asked Lemon, "Do you go on this way all the time?"

"Yeah. That's why we wouldn't let them come to the party. They take over, and the city folk think they're quaint and nobody else gets any attention."

By then a number of people had gathered, and some of the women asked, "Who made you all stay away?"

Both men said earnestly, "Lemon did it."

The women complained in shocked surprise, "Did you do that?"

And Lemon said, "Without turning a hair."

"Shame on you. How could you do that to these darling men?"

"Easy."

Margot added, "—ily."

Lemon said, "—ily."

Margot instructed, "You're supposed to add it to the word."

"Wordily."

The young morning hours were all that way, one way or the other. Clint and Charlie went out for their stint, and the hours did pass. In John's tux jacket, Margot did garner attention, and John had to shoulder and caution and give sobering stares to any number of men. It was good for John to be challenged and to be strained a little.

John had life much too easy, coping just with Lemon. That first morning of the new year widened John's talents. It was one of the burdens of the man to realize he gathered no points from Margot for his superb interference and blockings. She was unaware of most of his maneuvers.

And it occurred to John that with Lucilla, he'd never had to block or discipline other men around her. And he considered the two women. They were about as different as they could be.

Lucilla had been deliberately the Star, and Margot just included everyone around in having a good time.

She teased women as much as she taunted men. With her, even a blue norther would be fun for more than twenty minutes. She was really something. And John paid her more attention.

The change in John was apparent to Margot. She, too, was aware. She moved so that she was beside him. She didn't dance with anyone else. She wouldn't take off his jacket, as some men insisted. "I didn't see that dress. Come on. Take it off!" And there were whistles and hand clappings and coaxings.

It had been a long, long night and the entertainment was being stretched. So what was she to do? She looked around and saw a woman who was envious, and Margot said, "Don't you hear them? Go ahead!"

And the woman loved it. She laughed, she wiggled and pretended, and the men coaxed and teased. The whole climate changed. Other women were coaxed to pretend. And they laughed.

It was surprising how many of the women were really very good at moving and pretending. Margot clapped and whooped and exclaimed, but she didn't join the posturing others. She stayed by John.

It was during that time when she discovered John could play a musical instrument. The orchestra was barely back from their break when someone called for John to join them. "Come on, John, you have to do at least one song."

Margot asked John, "Do you play an instrument, too?"

And a voice replied, "Relentlessly. But he sulks if we don't let him do at least one piece when we have company. He's a show-off."

John laughed, shook his head and pretended not to want to play. But the Covington men were used to him, so they coaxed.

He said, "Now, fellas, you know what'll happen? I'll get involved with the music and ignore Margot, and she'll get peeved and feel neglected."

There were all sorts of volunteers for all sorts of distractions for Margot.

John asked, "See? What man can trust you buzzards?"

"Clint's gone!" They protested.

So they finally put a chair right in front, facing John's chair in the band. She was safely seated. And he played the spoons. Spoons! Yeah.

Nobody danced, they stood around and laughed and watched. He was very good, and he was earnest and smug. He got fancy, moving the spoons from one leg to the other, and with confidence and a touch of amused arrogance, he showed off...for her. He glanced to be sure she was watching him.

Margot loved it.

John only played one encore. Then he rose, and the band rose, too, and applauded. It was good fun.

When they could talk together, Margot said, "Such talent!"

"I have talents you haven't tapped."

She gave him a careful look, and he simply looked back.

He elaborated, "It'll take you a while to try them all."

She continued her carefulness, and he still watched her.

He said, "You haven't danced with me."

She grinned and opened her mouth.

"It's only one of the talents. There are the others."
And she was back to being careful.

He could dance. That was always a surprise. When males begin dancing, they are generally distracted and don't pay enough attention. Just holding a girl close is enough. But John could dance.

The sound of the storm intruded and it became cooler in the ballroom. The furnace and insulation were good under most circumstances, but the norther tried the limits. They were still comfortable. In fact, it was quite pleasant with all those hot bodies heating the big room. But the women came shivering back from the powder room and asked Lemon, "Do you have enough blankets?"

"You can always crawl in with me. I'd keep you warm."

It was really only then that John realized Lemon didn't have a woman there. And he wondered if Lemon had really expected Margot to be his partner when he'd gone up on her porch to convince her into coming for the weekend.

How does a winner ask the loser if he's taken his woman? How does he ask the loser if his woman didn't show up? What if Lemon hadn't had someone TO ask? And John felt uncomfortable. Until then, he hadn't even noticed that there was no partner for Lemon.

Did Lemon pine for Margot? He'd bought her that scandalous dress, and he'd talked and talked and talked to get her to accept it. Only after John had gone up onto the porch had Margot finally agreed to come for the weekend there at Cactus Ridge.

How does a man ask a friend if he's stolen his woman? She'd come into the library and locked the door. Lemon knew the library door had been locked. Had he searched for Margot? And John faced the fact that he couldn't/wouldn't give her back.

John had already branded her as his by putting her into his jacket. He hadn't made a conscious decision to do that. He'd just simply done it. She was his.

But it had been Clint who'd made John cover Margot with his jacket. He probably wouldn't have done that if it hadn't been for the lecherous Clint. That's why he'd covered her. It was then he'd realized other men would be looking at her just the way he looked at her.

How could she be so unaware of how she had looked in that nothing dress?

She wore his jacket. She stayed by him. She'd locked herself in the library with him and she'd waited for him when he'd gone to the lavatory. While he'd been gone, she could have escaped him. She could have gone back to the ballroom and not paid any more attention to him.

They could have been ships that had passed, signaled and gone on. John looked down at her beside him. She was watching the others dance. He said, "Margot."

She glanced up quickly with a slight smile.

She heated him. He said, "Can you hold up for another dance?"

"Mmm. You are so good! I love it that you refuse the other women who want to dance with you, but I know how they feel. You are really good."

"You're easy to lead. Not all women are."

"They don't get enough practice."

He'd taken her into his arms, and her comment caught his attention. He forgot what he was going to say. He wanted to kiss her. He was standing there, his arm was around her, holding her close. She had her arm around his shoulder and she was looking up, so he kissed her.

They came out of it to cheers and clappings and shouts of "Encore!" from men, and several females called, "Me next!"

Margot didn't notice. John glanced around, pleasant faced, and slowly shook his head at them all.

He moved her into the stream of dancers and looked down again. She was dazed. He did that to her. He asked, "Are you all right?"

"I'm wobbly."

He assured her with some smugness, "That's simple lust."

Since he'd discarded the magic as lust, she replied, "If it wasn't for lust, how could I tolerate your flaws?"

He slowly inquired, "Flaws?"

"Priscilla." Just the name was sufficient identification.

And she discovered that John could laugh in his throat exactly the way Clint had. It was a great talent for a man. That was when Margot proved she could look smug.

He offered in an expansive manner, "If you haven't paired up with anybody else, you could share my bed."

"How kind. But I have a bed."

"Where?"

"There are four of us in one of the attic rooms. It's bound to be cool up there. That's why I inquired about blankets."

"Four of you?" John questioned.

"That's all that caught your attention?"

He was sure. "The other three snore."

"You don't?"

"I've never noticed that I did. It would be a good opportunity for you to do research."

"My daddy has the perfect snore. Mama thanks God every once in a while—generally after we've had overnight company—that daddy's snore is just right."

"What sort of...overnight company?"

"All kinds. Kinfolk, friends, guests. Daddy's hip deep in politics. All kinds of people."

"Your...friends?"

"Sure."

"They come and spend the night?"

"Yeah."

"And..."

"And some don't snore at all. That would be unsettling. A man is supposed to snore discreetly so a woman doesn't feel she's alone."

"How could she feel alone in a house with a silent man?"

"It's when she hears a noise and is scared. If he snores, then she knows she's safe. If he wakens and jolts up, then she knows there's danger but he'll take care of it."

"How do you know all that?"

"Well, my mother told us all the important stuff all along! How else?"

He had to have it clarified. "You have men come sleep over at your family's house so you can test their snores?"

She explained, "My sisters. When they get serious, they do that."

"Uh. None of you has lived with anyone ahead of time?"

"Apparently not."

"Oh," he considered. "Just girls?"

"I beg your pardon." She looked down her nose at him.

"Uh, I meant were your parents exclusive of male offspring?"

"No, I have five brothers."

He considered that before he questioned, "And the sisters are plural?"

"I have only three sisters."

"I see."

She expanded his knowledge, "Mother kept thinking she could perfect the rhythm method. She said Daddy wasn't cooperative."

"Your house isn't—"

"I know. They couldn't find a house big enough without having a big ballroom—like this house—and parlors and living rooms and morning rooms and all that stuff. And those houses are too often like this one—out in the sticks. Where we lived, all the schools were within walking distance. So were grocery stores and bakeries and a branch library, all the needed things. And we have great neighbors."

"How'd you all fit into that house?"

"My brothers had the attic. We could hear smothered laughter and an occasional bump as they wrestled and played. Daddy would go up and sort them out if one yelled."

"We had a full house like that up in Ohio. Only it's like this one, and it's out on the edge of a little town. Most of the kids weren't actual kin. The Browns took in kids and adopted kids, and even now there're six under college age who live with them. It was nice, growing up there.''

"I think taking in kids would help. I'd like a big family, but I wouldn't necessarily have to actually give birth to them all.''

"Some of ours arrived by bus, some were brought by probation officers, some were dragged in by disgruntled relatives who wanted no part of them. And there were those forlorn ones who'd been abandoned.'' He paused thoughtfully. "Come to think of it, I don't believe anyone ever explained how kids get here. Did your mother explain the rhythm method to you?''

"No. She warned me about lechers who claimed they didn't know about sex.''

"One of those mothers.'' He was disgruntled.

"Fortunately.'' She was snippy.

He shook his head once. "Not necessarily.''

Five

With the music just perfect, the steps of the dance followed the acknowledged male dominance. He led. Margot tilted up her chin and looked at John. He swung her around in a lovely swirl and brought her back to him.

She looked at his mouth and observed the obvious. "I've never run into any man who is as forward as you. You're way ahead of yourself and shocking to an uninitiated woman."

"Uninitiated?"

"I've never tangled with a man."

He looked down into her smooth face on her sassily tilted head and told her, "With your tongue, you're about as wicked as a woman can be."

"I can't even touch the closest edge of Priscilla's...reputation."

He slowed to a dip, lifted her against him and turned her carefully. She knew exactly what he intended because he could lead perfectly. With him, no partner ever floundered or blundered. She felt selfish that she didn't encourage him to dance with other women so that they could know what a partner who knew what to do could do.

But he was still emerging from his zonked period of grief over Priscilla. Margot needed to lure him to her. She had wanted his attention for so long.

She remembered seeing him that first time and asking Lemon who he was. Lemon had replied, "He's a superior man. Right now he's stuck in a tar pit, but old Lucilla is out for bigger game and she'll dump him eventually."

Lemon had been right. Priscilla had finally rejected John. But he had suffered. Had he really loved that nasty woman? She looked up at the man dancing with her.

He saw the searching in her contemplative glance. His eyes held humor. His circling arm tightened. "I can't believe there are four virgins here to sleep chastely in the attic. Four virgins? Or are they four cautious women?"

"I can only speak for myself. Although I do know the other three, I don't know any of their personal history or preferences."

"You sound like a priggish woman."

"Exactly. What would make you surprised by that?"

"The dress you're wearing under my jacket."

"The dress is perfectly decent. You've been out of circulation too long, trailing after a waspy woman. Have you looked at the other dresses here?"

"No. I've only seen you."

"You must like red."

"I think it's the body inside the dress."

She nodded and confirmed his observation, "Female. You're a quick observer. In just one evening you've realized I'm female."

"You could wear a potato sack and make it the Thing to Wear."

"A compliment. Thank you."

"Or you could wear nothing at all and look easy... No, I don't mean that kind of easy. I mean you could look as if it were the normal thing to do."

"How come you're so fascinated by what I do or don't wear? Have you been brooding in solitude so long that you've forgotten it's nice to dance with women?"

"Partly."

"I think it would be a good idea if you dated around a little and became reacclimated."

"Who all would you suggest?" John's eyes were lazy as he slowly licked his lower lip and stood, swaying to the music, not distracting either of them with moving or following steps.

She looked around at the gorgeous laughing women who were charmingly tired from the long night, and their makeup and hair were a little in disarray. Just looking at one, a man could see how she'd look in bed, sleepy, smiling, friendly. Willing. Loose. Encouraging.

"I think all of these women are taken." She looked up into his eyes with candor.

But he laughed. He hugged her and laughed.

She got snippy. "I believe it's time for me to admit this night is finished."

"Already?"

"It's almost six. Have you noticed there aren't very many people around? The other three sharing my room are already gone. I ought to go up. This has been a wonderful evening. Thank you. I have had such a nice time. You're a fine man. I love your humor—and your tolerance. You've been very kind to me."

He bowed his head slightly to acknowledge her compliments. "You're good company. You have a way to go before you're smoothed out, but you're trainable."

"Uh-oh."

He was rather elaborately startled. "Did I allow some slippage there? Shucks."

"You're probably a lot closer to Clint than I would suspect."

"Clint?"

She shared common knowledge. "He's a prairie wolf."

"You were alert enough, after my kiss, for you to realize that?"

"The alarm bells went off."

"Smoke alarm?"

"Mother-training gongs. No mother sends an innocent daughter out into the wilds of civilization without some guidelines. Clint is all the things women are warned about."

John chided, "Clint's a good man."

"To another man. For women, he's very dangerous."

John frowned. "Now, why's that?"

"How would I know? I just know if you don't want to get in trouble, you avoid men like Clint."

"And I'm safe?" He almost concealed his pretended indignation. It was well done.

She could see he was cheekily offended, but she couldn't stop the laugh. "You've been on the stage."

"No, but my adoptive mother is."

"Osmosis." She agreed his background fitted what she knew of him. "And now you're practicing to become a prairie wolf?"

"No, not entirely, I'm too old for playing that game much longer. I'm about eight years older than you. I've been out and around. I do find it irks me that you find Clint dangerous, and you didn't mind being in a locked library with me for several hours. You felt safe? That's offensive to any red-blooded American male."

Her laughter bubbled. She kept her mouth closed, but her shoulders shook so her breasts were probably jiggling under that jacket, and the lights in her eyes danced so charmingly.

"I'm going to kiss you good-night and then we'll just see who you find dangerous."

Her giggles stopped and her eyes were again three inches high and two and a half wide.

He noted that with some smugness. He said, "Come on, woman, I'm taking you to your room. You'll need the rest."

"The 'rest' of what?"

"See? Your mother may have explained the rhythm method and why you should cross your legs, but she neglected to curb your sassy tongue. Have you ever talked that way in front of your mother?"

"She always explained things. She would have said, 'You need to rest.' You said, 'You need the rest.' There's a difference in word choice."

"Are you an English major?"

"No. I'm a stickler."

John sighed. "I can sure as hell agree to that. You've spent the whole evening lecturing me and testing me and tempting me. You're a— I'll explain after breakfast."

"Are you a grouch before breakfast?"

"No. I waken alert and ready."

"See? There's another. Ready...for what?"

He looked at her soberly. "Whatever you want."

She kept her eyes on him, but her body betrayed her. She shivered and put her arms around herself as the excitement quivered in her body. She said, "I'll go on up."

"Up...what?"

"The stairs to the room in the attic to which I am assigned."

"I'll escort you."

She didn't object, but she did glance around. Apparently the orchestra had left some time before because the music was from a tape player that had amplifiers. There weren't too many people left around. There were more men than women, and the women were surrounded very like a victim with the buzzards who weren't quite still.

Lemon was gone. Knowing Lemon, he'd be out in that storm checking on his men. Even Margot knew that. The pair left the room, and there were glances which trailed after them. Margot was tempted to turn back and say, "No, we're not."

Since such a protest did sound as if she was thinking of going to bed with John, she kept quiet.

As they climbed the first flight of the grand stair, John said, "You could share my bed. I can be trusted." And he said, "I wouldn't touch you if you didn't want me to." And on the landing, he paused and said, "I have control." And going up the next segment of stairs, he urged, "You'd be safe."

On the lesser staircase to the attic, he said, "I've never taken an unwilling woman." On that landing, he said earnestly, "You can trust me. I can keep you warm without making love to you...I think. Possibly. Well—maybe."

She snorted.

"You're just not an accepting female. You could become an irritation."

And she laughed.

They came to the attic hallway. He started to say something else, but under the sound of the furious storm, she whispered, "Shh. They're all asleep."

He stopped in the open doorway as she fumbled with the designated night-light. She said, "Turn alien again."

"You want to demonstrate the *s-e-x?*"

"No. Aliens glow in the dark." She looked at him impatiently and complained, "You're not glowing."

"I do under the covers."

"Shh! They'll be asleep."

She found the light and turned it on. The two intruders looked at the beds. They were neatly made. No one else was there.

She said, "Thank you for the escort."

"I'll just stick around until the other ladies arrive. I don't like leaving you alone up here."

"There's no need. I'll close the door."

"And lock it."

"I only lock library doors."

"Come down to my room."

"That was part of the agreement with Lemon on my front porch. I wasn't going to share your room."

"That's so narrow-minded. You know you can trust me. I wouldn't lay a finger on you," he said as she gasped. "What's with the word lay, to make you gasp that way?"

"It's cold up here."

"You're shivering! Now how can you get into a cold bed all by yourself? You come down to my room. I guarantee you'll be warmer."

"I have flannel pajamas."

John spat the words, "Some old maid who hated men invented flannel paja— How come you talked about sleeping with me to Lemon on your front porch?"

"He wanted to know if I would share your room."

"My God! You two were— We'd just met! Or was your conversation even before I caught my first glimpse of you? You two had it all planned out? Weren't you invited here by Lemon? Weren't you supposed to be his date?"

She said, "No," as she handed him his jacket and he got to see the dress again. It was a scandal. Why was it such a scandal? It did cover her. It was red. Red was for bull men. It clung to her, and when she breathed it showed her chest sparkling sinfully. How could a chest be sinful just by breathing? Hers was.

He'd missed some of her conversation and got in on her saying, "This wasn't your 'first glimpse' of me. I've been seeing you all through the last almost two years. You just couldn't 'see' me. I suppose you don't remember being my partner at bridge in Galveston? You trumped my ace."

As he took off his tie and put it into his jacket pocket, he protested, "I *never* trumped an ace!" Opening his shirt, he frowned as he considered she was serious. He offered, "I must have only had trumps."

"You weren't paying attention. Priscilla was laughing over at another table with some other man. You were watching them."

"I would never have trumped an ace. My stepmother, Felicia, taught me bridge. She was a stickler. She said never trump a partner's ace a hundred thousand times. It was only surpassed by the rule that one must follow suit."

She said, "I've got to brush my teeth. This has been a wonderful New Year. Thank you."

"My pleasure. I can't believe I'd ever trump a partner's ace."

"Good night."

"Yeah."

At the bathroom door, Margot looked back, and John was standing in the empty hall, rubbing the back of his neck. She turned away, wishing she could do it for him. Rub him and make him sigh in contentment.

She brushed her teeth and washed her face. She ran a warm cloth over her body and gave up. She was getting so sleepy....

Having put on the flannel pajamas, she swung the robe around her shoulders, picked up her discarded clothing and slid her feet into her lined slippers.

She opened the door to a cold hallway. She wanted to get to bed before she chilled, so she hurried down the hall and into the room—to find John stretched out on the bed.

He started to rise, "Through?"

"Yes." She put her clothes in her closet and turned back. He was delaying her getting immediately into bed. She was getting chilled.

"You look twelve."

"I'm more than twice that. Good night."

"I get a kiss."

Uh-oh. But she couldn't not have one from him. She wanted one. Or maybe two. She smiled just a tiny bit.

He got up and hugged her. He stood with her against him, and she realized the robe was on the floor. He said, "You smell so nice. I'm glad you didn't take a shower."

"How'd you know that?"

"You didn't wash your hair."

"It would have frozen into icicles."

"I'd thaw you."

Mmm-hmm, she thought.

"I'll just get your bed warm." He sat down on the bed and lifted the covers, moving over. His shoes were on the floor by her bed.

She closed her eyes against the tide of temptation. "You must not."

"I don't understand your problem in this. I'm only concerned that you'll freeze to death up here. Whoever thought there'd be a blue norther at this time of year."

"It's a logical time."

He allowed the covers to cover him. He lay on his side, watching her. He reminded her, "I'm here to get you warm. Quit standing there in the cold and let me do it."

"I'm not too sure you aren't another Clint. You could coax me into bed to warm me, and then what would you do?"

"Whatever you wanted."

She took a deep, patient breath.

He said softly, "I'll bet those alarm gongs you're hearing are an echo from your meeting Clint."

"No. They are all yours."

"Come here and give them back to me."

She scoffed. "You want to be alarmed?"

"Please, oh, please!"

And she laughed.

"Okay, it's warm. Get in quick." He lifted the covers. "Hurry!"

She got in. Just like that. Mindlessly. She got into bed with him. And he was hot. He was better than a hot-water bottle. Better than a heating pad. He covered more space.

He enclosed her. He breathed fire. He pulled her against him and put his hot feet under her cold ones and he groaned. Then he kissed her.

His mouth sought hers, he rooted around until she lifted her mouth in surrender. His mouth took hers. His lips were hot to her chilled lips. He seemed to eat at her mouth and he made savoring sounds. He excited her.

She pried her reluctant face from his and said a breathless, "Good night."

He laughed in his throat in that awful, luring way.

Hearing his laugh, she asked, "Are you going to give me a hard time?"

His breaths were a little harsh. "I sure hope so."

"Listen, John, you aren't supposed to be in my bed. You're supposed to go down and sleep in your own."

"And leave you up here all by yourself? No way. I'm your protection."

Very softly, she asked, "Who protects me from you?"

He went still. Then he drew his head back a little so that he could look at her. He asked in a vulnerable voice, "Don't you want me?"

"I know you very well. I've known you for a long time. But, John, you don't know me. You had never even noticed me before you met me on my front porch. So you recognized me here, just last night."

"Does it irritate you that I never recognized you? Is that what this is about?"

"No. I just think you ought to be sure before you fool around with me. I could be hurt by your carelessness. I want us to go more slowly."

"You're a holdout."

"Yes. Sex is important. I don't just want sex. That's easy. When I give you my body to love, I want it to be important, not just release."

"When..."

"I plan to snare you. But I want you willing."

"Hell, woman, I'm about as willing as a man can get!"

"For sex. I want love."

"You sure know how to make it hard for a guy."

"I didn't do anything."

"You wore that dress."

"Good grief! That dress wasn't wicked. It's a perfectly decent dress!" She got out of bed and went over to her closet and took out the dress. She shook it out and held it up to her and frowned at him, annoyed. "See?" She spread it over the flannel pajama top and held it to one hip. "Do you see? It's perfectly okay!"

"You're right. It's your body that's the scandal."

"Baloney!" Standing in the flannel pajamas, she held out her arms and said, "See?"

Smoldering on the bed, he suggested, "Take off the pajamas and let's see the basic woman."

"I'm not that foolish."

"Come back to bed. You'll catch cold out there."

And darned if she didn't crawl right back in with him! He gathered her to him and kissed her again. She shivered in his arms, and he chided, "See? You got cold out there." His big, hot hands ran over her, crowding her closer to him.

She whispered, "I'm shivering because I want you."

He went absolutely still. "Margot?"

"No."

"But you said—"

She was sure. "I can wait."

"I'm not sure I can."

"How can I help you do it by yourself?"

"You'd do that?"

She moved her hands. "Yes. I know it hurts."

He caught her hand. "Hell." He considered carefully. "I can wait if you can." Then he asked, "How long? Fifteen minutes?"

She chuckled, lifting her hand to waggle his head.

Her move opened her body, and he pulled her closer. He pressed against her and groaned in agony.

She whispered, "Oh, John. I can't tell you the times I dreamed of you being in bed with me."

"Let me make it real."

She laughed softly in his ear, and he about crushed her in his arms.

He said, "You're driving me crazy."

"I think you just want sex. You don't know me well enough to want to make love."

"I make quick decisions."

And unfairly, she reminded him, "I interrupted your melancholy reluctance to face a new year without that awful woman."

"Are you going to dust her off for the rest of our lives? I thought you said I couldn't mention that twenty years from now, and here you bring it up in just a couple of hours...well, it's been better than nine hours since you made the rule. Do you realize we've spent almost twelve hours together? That's worth three dates. Wouldn't you be a little friendlier in three dates?"

"I have. You've kissed me in a very unhello-like way. And your hands have been very curious about me."

"Did you notice that? I thought I was pretty clever in being careless."

"You've been doing that since you put your head on my lap."

"What a view."

"See? You don't love me, you simply want to couple with me."

"Is that what they mean by couples? They are a couple because they couple?"

"Probably. How did your hand get there?"

"I was just checking for female traits."

"Cut it out."

"You're hot! You want me!"

"I've already told you that."

"But I know it! You weren't just saying it to salve my ego, you really do want me. You're not just submitting to allow—"

"Submitting?" She frowned.

"Yeah. Tease a man crazy and then give up even when you don't want to."

"Who did that?"

"Uh— Admit you want me," he coaxed.

"I've alre—"

"Kiss me and say it to me," his voice was intense.

"I'm not sure it would be wise."

"I have protection for you."

She was surprised. "When did you get it?"

"When I went to the men's lav."

"There's a dispenser there? What a den of iniquity!"

"Well, there's the need. Where're your three roomies?"

"They're in that last lingering bunch?"

Again, he urged, "Kiss me and tell me you want me."

"I'm beginning to sweat. You're like an oven."

"Let me get out of these pants." He moved to do that, lying flat, unzipping and sliding them as he shifted.

She was still protesting, "No!"

He flung the pants over her, onto the floor by his shoes. "There. It'll cool me off."

"Your pants make you hot?"

"Without them, I'm cooler."

She became cautious. "I'm not sure that's good."

"You want me hot!"

"No. I think you ought to have them on."

"What?"

"Your pants."

''You want to take them off for me? Honey, I don't think I'd last. You'd fool around and explore— Here, hug me.''

She said, ''Now, John—''

And he kissed her with a steaming, scorching, debilitating kiss. His hot hand was up under her pajama top, moving over her, touching and rubbing and kneading her breasts.

The rough skin of his palm was a contrast to the soft skin on the inside of her thigh. His palm was that of a working man. How could it be? He was a horseback rider; he was a physical man. She couldn't prevent a sensuous body-response to his hand.

He unbuttoned her pajama top and ducked his head under the covers. His mouth caressed her, nuzzling her. His mouth found her nipple and she gasped, going rigid. His hands soothed and petted her and he made purring sounds. He came up her body and found her mouth and kissed her the double-whammy killer kiss. She was lost.

He cherished her. His hands and mouth relished her. He held her to him and gasped with the feel of her against his naked body.

They were naked! She stiffened. He made comforting sounds as he smoothed his hands over her. His kisses became gentle and sweet. He simply loved her with his arms, with his mouth and hands—holding, touching, caressing, feeling and being very intimate, but he didn't make love to her.

She moved and indicated she would accept him. She gasped and shifted, but he didn't take her. He touched and nuzzled. He stroked and explored. He was gentle and sweet, and he made pleasured sounds of appreciation. But he didn't make love with her.

He finally held her so that she couldn't possibly move and he patted her head with one hand as he said, "Shh." And he calmed himself as he held her immobile.

She was still. She didn't know why he was being so quiet. She listened to hear if someone was coming upstairs. Wouldn't he get out of her bed? What if one of the other three women was to come in and find John in bed with her? It would shock her. The other woman would probably be shocked, too.

And she heard his first gurgle of a snore. He swallowed, relaxed more comfortably and settled a little more; then he went soundly to sleep. He was ASLEEP!

She couldn't believe it. Here she was willing, wanting to help, and he had gone to sleep! Not only that, she was wide-awake and wild! She needed...she wanted...she was... And she almost laughed out loud.

She jiggled with her smothered giggles. His perfect snore faltered and his hands soothed her minutely.

Then she was suddenly sobered. How many times had Priscilla lain in his arms that he automatically held a woman this tightly? And black jealousy filled Margot with a terrible bile.

Six

During that sleep, Margot had the most marvelous dreams of loving and caring, of no longer being a separate entity. Even in the middle of her big family, she'd always known she belonged somewhere else. And even dreaming, and knowing that she dreamed, it was a wondrous feeling.

But then in that sleep, she dreamed of separateness. She was no longer whole and she wakened to an empty bed. She was alone. When had John left her?

How could her subconscious be so aware of another when she was used to being alone? How could her subconscious so quickly adapt to John being with her? Was it an omen? She would share her life—for a while—then he would leave?

She lay brooding, thinking, and she knew that even if it was for only a while, she would share her life with John. However little time he gave to her, it would be worth anything at all. And it was better than nothing....

Nonsense. That was a sober foolishness. But it was true. She would do it. She would take what she could have of his magic. He'd probably felt the same way about that awful woman who'd mesmerized him all that while.

What a stupid woman Priscilla was to leave John. What was it about her that had snared him so tightly? What magic had Priscilla possessed that she could capture his regard?

Margot thought if she could stand to just look at Priscilla, she would be an interesting study.

And she recalled John had been in the isolated library so that he could mourn the past year in which he'd been Priscilla's lover. How long ago had they split? Split? Priscilla had abandoned him. It had been last spring. Could a man grieve for an indifferent lover for so long a time?

How could another woman hope to replace someone like Priscilla? What had the woman done to deserve such devotion?

Margot lay quietly, the thick quilt that covered her kept her cozy. The other beds were neat and made up. Had her roomies never come up to bed? Or had they slept and gone again? Margot gazed out the far window across the room beyond the sofa. Her mind didn't register the cold sky.

The storm was past. The winds still blew, and the sky wasn't so dangerous.

What time was it? All she had to do was lift her hand from under the quilt and look at her watch. She wasn't curious enough.

She could hear laughter far away. Someone was outside. More than someone, no one alone laughs that way. Margot was glum.

There was a light tap on her open door. One of her roommates? She lifted her head to glance at the door and there stood John. John.

He was dressed in denims and looked as good in them as he'd looked in the tuxedo. He was serious. In his hand was a cup of coffee. "Are you awake?"

"Almost."

"You snored loud enough to shake all the snow off the roof. Lemon says to thank you."

She covered her head with the top quilt.

His weight dipped the bed. "If you sit up very carefully, I'll let you have some of my coffee."

She was still naked. "I don't know where my pajamas are."

He bit into his lower lip and straightened his back as he breathed brokenly. "My God, woman, what a thing to say to a man who is being very careful."

She moved up on one elbow, and her bare shoulders were only minimally exposed to his view, but the cold air slid in right between her back and those warm sheets. She said, "Brr!" and lay back down.

"I'll get your robe."

"A sweater in the top drawer."

"Please!" He looked at her indignantly.

She smiled a cat's smile. "Please."

"Your momma may have told you about the rhythm method, but she sure neglected your manners. It wasn't an hour after I went to sleep that you burrowed under me and pushed me right out of your bed!"

"Never!"

"Yep."

"You don't talk Ohioan."

"Honey chile, I've been down in these here parts for ten years yesterday. That means I've been a Texican for a whole ten years! Now, you gotta know that Ohio isn't like that. They still call your place by the person who first owned it. My adoptive father, Salty, bought a big, old, broken-down house on ten acres of land that had been owned by the Indians but had been bought by a family named Tilby. The last Tilby died a long time ago and the house had been owned by other people, but it is STILL the Tilbys'."

"In Texas, we just mention how many generations our family's been here. I'm a sixth generationer."

He nodded to show her he'd understood that. Then he said, "When you said you were going to retir—"

"Don't say it! Don't you say it! I've heard that all my life and I know it by heart! How long have you been using that?"

He was astonished and reacted quite elaborately. "Let's see. I learned 'fair to middling,' which is pronounced 'far to mid'lin.' I learned about calling ladies 'ma'am' and then it was 'shucks,' which had to be some farmer's word and not a cattleman's saying." He got a sweater from the drawer and noted the mirror next to the bureau. He went to the bed and held the sweater above her head. He witnessed her struggling into it while holding the blankets to her chest.

He chided her, "You're a selfish woman." He *tsk*ed once. Then he watched her as he continued. "I learned to call a gun an 'iron,' and I think it was right in there somewheres—note the *S* on that one—that I learned about retiring for the night. No. I learned 'How's that?' before then."

"It must be a real pain to learn to be a Texan."

"Yep. 'Real pain' was in there somewhere."

"—s."

"—s. Then there's 'Now I'll tell you—' and of course 'they's,' 'honey' and 'I swear to goodness' and—"

"Good grief."

"Yep. And 'little ole' and—"

Very discreetly arranging the sweater, she warned him, "You get used to the talk down here and you'll never pass for an Ohioan when you go back up yonder."

"Yonder. That's another of the passel of local talk."

"Hush."

"Yeah, I just about forgot that'un."

She held her head.

"You get a little too much red-eye last night, sugar?"

"Give me the coffee."

"Say please. I lugged it all the way up all those steep old stairs."

"Well, I'll be danged."

"Honey chile, you getting mouthy on me?"

And she laughed.

The coffee was perfect. He helped arrange the pillows behind her, before he sat on the bed alongside hers. She could tell he was thinking wickedly because his eye crinkles were deep and his lips fought his smile . . . almost.

So she ignored him and sipped the delicious brew. No cream, no sugar. She sighed. But it was good. She didn't mention the lacks. He'd be determined to go back for those, and she preferred to have him there, looking at her.

GOOD NEWS! You can get up to FIVE GIFTS—FREE!

If offer card is missing, write to:
Silhouette Reader Service, P.O. Box 609, Fort Erie, Ontario L2A 5X3.

MAIL POSTE

Canada Post Corporation / Société canadienne des postes

Postage paid
If mailed in Canada

Port payé
si posté au Canada

Business
Reply

Réponse
d'affaires

0195619199   01

0195619199-L2A5X3-BR01

SILHOUETTE READER SERVICE
PO BOX 609
FORT ERIE ON   L2A 9Z9

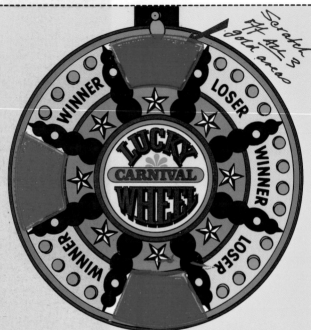

Scratch all 3 goth areas

YES! I have scratched off the 3 Gold Areas above. Please send me all the gifts for which I qualify. I understand I am under no obligation to purchase any books, as explained on the opposite page.

326 CIS ANDP
(C-SIL-D-01/94)

NAME

ADDRESS   APT.

CITY   PROV.   POSTAL CODE

She would raise her eyes, and he'd still be watching her.

He told her, "You're a miracle, do you realize that? I've never before been allowed to sleep with a woman, alone that way. It was wonderful."

"Why did you leave me?"

The quick intake of his breath was audible as he reacted to her wording. Then he explained, "When there's a rallying call for help, the gong's struck once. You can respond or not. If it's struck more than that, everybody rallies. In the night, it was a one-gonger. We had to go out and rescue a stuck bull. He was trapped in some ice. We needed to get him out so he wouldn't freeze his . . . feet."

"Is rescuing stuck bulls part of your job description?"

"I have to watch out for Lemon or we're all out of jobs. That mule-headed man doesn't realize he's mortal."

She knew that wasn't the reason. John was simply a caretaker and he'd committed to taking care of Lemon's money, and that included watching out for Lemon. "The storm's stopped." She gestured.

He didn't need to look. "It's cool outside. There's snow. Want to go out and play?"

"Yes!"

"Good. I brought you a sandwich." He reached into his pocket and handed her a very large cloth napkin. Then he carefully took out a paper-wrapped egg-and-bacon sandwich on homemade bread. It was a bit crumbly, but it was WONDERFUL!

He watched her eat and lick around her mouth and say a lot of *mmm*'s. He laughed at her and said, "Are you like that when you make love?"

"I don't know."

"We'll find out."

A remarkable slithering thrill went through her stomach and she looked at him with eyes that were again three inches high and two and a half wide.

"Can't wait, can you? But you have to be patient. I'm courting you, right and proper."

"Are you going to turn into one of those professional Texans who is worse than a real one?"

"More than likely."

"Lord save us."

"Hallelujah!"

She protested, "It's simply too early in the morning for this conversation."

"Honey, it's clear past noon. And I 'spect any time of the day or night, strugglin' this'a way, might be a burden."

"No doubt. I do hope, by now, that you've learned you all or y'all isn't said to specify one person?"

"It took a while. Come on, sugar, get your sweet self out of that there bed and get some clothes on your precious body. If you don't hustle up and get out of that bed, I'm a-gonna get in with you and you'll never get to play in the snow."

"I'll meet you downstairs."

He was offended. "I came up here to help you. How can I do that from clear down those long flights of stairs I struggled up, just so as you could have some caffeine? I ought to at least get to watch you get out of bed. That's a long sweater. It's about as long as last night's dress."

"There you go again! There is nothing wrong with that dress!"

"When we have our passel of young'uns, I don't want you to ever show them that there dress. You could ruin their young minds and set them on the road to degradation."

Through her teeth, sitting straight and leaning forward, she said, "That dress is perfectly all right."

"On anniversaries, we'll send the kids to Salty and Felicia, and you can wear it for me in the privacy of our own home."

"No woman deliberately lives with a man who is as prejudiced against good clothing as you appear."

"I didn't know you wanted to live in sin. I coulda stayed last night if I'd'a known that! How come you didn't mention last night that you didn't mind living in sin and having kids! You'll shock Salty and Felicia."

"Well, you hadn't mentioned marriage."

"I sure enough did, last night."

"I don't recall that."

"You were hotter than a two-dollar pistol and clawing at me and wiggling around—" He stood up and pushed his hands into his jeans pockets. "I can't remember like that or I'll go berserk."

"I'll meet you downstairs."

"You have to kiss me first." He turned and just eased the coffee cup from her hand. He tucked the napkin into the top of her sweater with a whole lot of preciseness, and he sat beside her and kissed her witless.

If that was one kiss, it went on for a long, searching, busy time. His breathing was erratic and he trembled, but he did let her go very carefully.

She sank back down onto her pillow and closed her eyes.

He leaned over her. "Honey? Margot? Are you all right?"

Through uncertain lips, she whispered, "We need a warning label on you."

He became indignant. He straightened up and complained, "On ME? I was perfectly all right until you kissed me. I was a functioning human. I've turned into a raving maniac who has a leaning to ravaging. You have to be more careful how you kiss me."

"I won't."

He frowned at her. "Does that 'won't' mean you won't kiss me wickedly, or you won't be careful of me."

Her eyes still closed, her lips managed, "Whatever."

"Now that makes no sense at all!"

Crossly, she complained, "How can you kiss me and then have the organization to debate? You're impossible."

"Oh, now, that's not true a-tall. Of all the men you have handy around these here parts, and without question I'm the most possible of them all. Try me."

She took a patient breath and looked out at the sky. "I was lying here in bed, reasonably contented and peaceful, and you came in."

"I really joggle your libido, right?"

She looked at him and gave an impatiently brief sigh, which just missed being a soundless snort. "You are making me argumentative. My mother would gasp in shock."

"Would she know you were stark, staring naked when I came in and helped you put on a skimpy sweater?"

"Her hair would turn gray."

His lashes came down over his wicked eyes and he said softly, "I met your gray-haired momma about a month ago when the Christmas lights were turned on in San Antone."

"Do you know that most of the people who mispronounce that city's name are not from there? Most people from San Antonio say it like that."

"Are we having another session of Talking Texan?"

"Everyone who lives in this great state is a part of the state chamber of commerce. It's on our birth certificates?" That was a do-you-understander. "It's like knowing you never turn watch hands backward when you're setting it."

"Oh."

"Just . . . oh?"

"I want you to get out of bed whilst—that's another important word—whilst I can watch."

She considered. There was no reason for him to have to see her get out of bed. It was none of his business whether she did or didn't. She would obey his demand to watch because she wanted him to watch her. That was simple enough.

As John had mentioned, the sweater was long enough. It covered her hips. But the idea of carefully getting out of a warm bed and standing in a drafty room, without any underwear, was something to consider. An air-cooling bottom would remind her how hot he made her.

It wasn't any big project to get out of bed, but she was a tease. So she did it elaborately. She licked her lower lip several times, as she geared her courage. Then she squirmed a little, being sure the garment was down enough. And she moved to the edge of the bed, glancing to be sure she had his attention.

She did.

So she put her feet to the woolly bedside rug, and clutching the quilts to her stomach, she stood up. Then she turned and gave John a very smug look as her other hand straightened the bottom of her sweater. It wasn't hers. It was shorter. It barely covered her bottom. Her mouth opened and she gasped . . . as he reached and yanked away the quilt.

She instantly grasped the front of the sweater and leaned forward to pull it down hard—forgetting the mirror in back of her. "You're a beast!"

He stood there and smiled and smiled and smiled as she protested. She sank down onto the rug and scolded him as a cretin as she tried to stretch the bottom of the sweater over vital parts.

He flopped across the bed and reached to drag her to the side of it, and he kissed her until her head spun around.

It was another remarkable encounter. Maybe he really was from outer space. She'd never been kissed like that by any other man. Of course, she'd never been teased as John teased her, and she'd never been forced to kneel/sit on a rug trying to cover her bottom with an inadequate sweater.

His hands around her head, he pulled back only enough so that she had to look cross-eyed to see him. He said, "Give up."

"You're a wicked man."

"A man does as he must."

"It's 'Ya gotta do wha'cha gotta do.'"

"Similar."

"A Texan would say, 'close.'"

"Close." Then he kissed her again. His roughened breathing as he lifted his mouth and the tiny sounds as he licked his lips and swallowed were all so hungry. His voice was reedy as he said, "I gotta get outta here. See if you can get dressed by yourself. I can't handle any more."

She didn't reply. She sat there, toppled off her heels, curled against the bed, holding down the sweater, and she just looked at him.

He chided, "You set hard rules."

She nodded minutely.

He rolled over and got off the bed. He shoved his hands into his jeans pockets as he walked slowly to the door of the room, and he looked back from there. But he didn't say anything for a minute. He just looked at her. Actually, he looked beyond her to the mirror. Then he said, "I'll be sitting on the bottom step at the entrance hall."

She nodded.

He smiled, slowly shook his head once and left the room. The sounds of his boots went down the hall to the stairs and clattered down those.

She got up cautiously. Then she hurried, got her clothes, and peeking quickly both ways out the door, went down the hall to the bath.

Since they'd be going outside, she was careful not to get her hair wet. She got into the shower, rinsed off and found the towel bar was heated. Nice.

With Lemon's place being where it was, and as isolated as it was, their weekend entertainment could quite possibly be on horseback or tramping. So Margot had brought along jeans, a lined jacket and boots. And of course a Stetson.

Since John had brought her the coffee-and-sandwich breakfast in bed, she dressed for the out-of-doors and went down the stairs. John was where he'd said he'd be, except as soon as he heard her steps, he stood up to watch her come down the stairs. He protested, "You changed!"

And she laughed. He blocked her from leaving the stairs and required a toll charge to get past. Since she had no change on her, and he wouldn't accept a promissory note, he took a kiss.

She pretended great shock and indignation. She said that even Clint had better manners, and John was offended.

They went out and viewed the snow sculptures, which a practiced lake-effect snow-veteran Ohioan could criticize with esthetic complaints about amateurs. He did that stoically through all their derision.

One woman said, "Honey, this is TEXAS snow? All caps. And that's a do-you-understand statement. Remember that. And this here snow just don't bind the way the Chicago-polluted Ohio snow does. This stuff is the pure atomic-residue-tainted real thing."

The debate went on and on. Lemon claimed he paid the inept Yankee, John Brown, just as a conversational stimulator for bored TEXANS so they could get in all the old clichés.

John gasped in admiration. "You know cliché right out loud? Mercy to goodness!"

Lemon denied being unique. "I got that there word from you. You use it all out and about."

Even Margot held her head over that one.

So the two finally went to the barn and got the riding horses saddled. They rode out, admiring the fast-melting Texas snow. John knew the territory, so Lemon was freed to do something else.

Margot turned and watched the landmarks. John saw that she did and asked, "You think I'm dragging you out into the brush to get you lost so as you'll be compromised by having to spend the night out, lost, with a wicked and sinful man."

"Yep."

"God, there's nothing worse than a smart woman." He looked at her, disgruntled.

She licked her lips and lowered her eyelids in a very smug manner.

"No heart at all," he complained.

With especially polite interest, she asked, "Why aren't you riding the pinto?"

"It *was* suggested. He does need to be exercised, but all the guys are tired after last night's storm. Don't think for a minute they were kind about trying to get me to ride that damned pinto. They even said they'd splash him with a brown covering—they had handy in the barn—so I wouldn't realize what I was on. That way, I'd be confident and not so edgy when I rode him, and he'd be kind. I did see through such an argument . . . and right away."

"You ride well. Did you learn in Ohio?"

"We had an unridable pony that's still unridable. I didn't learn about horses until about four years ago. It was not easy. These guys are all jokesters. They put me on the pinto first."

"It's a wonder it didn't break your neck."

"Well, you see, they'd already taught me how to fall. They excused doing it by mentioning gopher holes and rattlers and those kinds of things. So when the— horse—pitched me the first time, I did land okay. I limped a while but nothing broke."

"But you were the only one who could get him to jump the fence."

"As I've mentioned, that horse does just exactly as he chooses. And when he doesn't choose, it's unexpected. I'll never know how I got over that fence . . . with him . . . while I was still on his back and still actually in the saddle."

"The guys here have a rough sense of humor." Margot looked at John, curious as to how he'd respond.

"They're a good bunch. I've seen such tenderness with a hurt man. Rough language and chiding and quarreling, and their touches so careful as they give him help and get him help."

"You're hooked."

"You know Lemon. He's a superior man. I hope I can stay with him. He's so sharp and so interested, and money isn't important. It's living. He's a superior liver of his life, and he spreads the gladness of it to us all."

"How could you have been lured by Priscilla? If Lemon had shown you the joy of living, why did you choose that trial?"

"I hadn't met you."

She contemplated him in irritation, but he was looking off to the horizon. Was he thinking of his grief for Priscilla? Was he anguished by—

He said, "Look at the colors. I never really noticed them until my sister Carol went to art school. One summer I was home, and she was there painting. I didn't have anything to do, so I lay back in the lazy grass in the shade and watched her paint. She does it perfectly. The shadings of color. It was a one-day lesson in seeing."

"Is she a painter?"

"She's a painterly painter. The top. She's in Chicago and married just recently to a retired police detective who writes horror books."

"Now there's a contrast."

And John said with satisfaction, "They balance."

"Do we?"

"Of course."

"In what way?"

He smiled just the slightest bit and slid a glance over to her. "We both like me."

She put back her head and laughed. She heard her own laugh, and it was very like the sound of laughter she'd heard outside when she was in bed. She had known the one laughing wasn't alone. And Margot now understood the woman had been with a man she liked.

They went quite a way, and the day was closing down. John took Margot to a line shack. There was a windmill and a water tower. On the other side of the shack, there was a horse shed. It was enclosed on three sides with the south side open. There were two horses there.

Two men came from the shack calling greetings. They were Ned and Jasper. "You okay?"

"Yep." John sat easily, waiting for the invitation to dismount.

"Light and visit." They were welcoming. "We just set down to supper." The two riders were especially welcomed since one was a woman.

With a grin, one of the men said, "You get to eat with us. Now you can see what real cowboys eat."

Cautiously, Margot inquired, "What are you having?"

In astonishment the men asked, "Is there something else besides beans?"

And they exclaimed and demanded to be told what else people ate, if it weren't beans.

All the while, they were holding Margot's stirrup and elbow and helping her down and telling John, "You'll be here a while, unsaddle and give those poor, tired horses some grain."

They took Margot into the shack. They hung her coat on a wall peg, and she removed her gloves and put them in a coat pocket as she hung her hat on the peg. Then she looked around.

The shack consisted of one room with a black iron stove in the middle, bunks along the wall and a table and chairs to one side.

The two called her "Miss," and Margot realized John hadn't introduced them. She wondered why. And it surprised her such formal conduct was still lurking in the peripheral sections of the country.

She felt a lick of unease when she saw a brace had been put against the door. What was going on?

John came to the door, crashed it open with his booted foot and walked inside as if one always came into a room that way.

The two apologized profusely for closing the door on John. "Didn't even see you, boy."

"Couldn't let the heat out." Then, to Margot, "You warm enough, honey?"

And the other was logical. "We didn't actually— lock—the door. That little bitty stick couldn't keep a big man like you out of here, now could it? And the door does tend to sag."

And they said, "Staying the night, honey? We need the warmth. With you between Ned and me, we'd be just real cozy."

John said, "Now, boys—"

And they laughed. "Sit down. Sit down. Here, let's move the table over, and Jasper'll use the bed. Just three chairs, and John probably wouldn't want to sit on your lap, honey."

She inquired, "How long have you two been out here?"

"Almost twenty-four...hours. You thought I was going to say days, didn't you. Naw. We got here just before the storm hit, and we've been watching to be sure the cattle's okay. Have some bread. Made it myself. It's good for sopping up the gravy. Like that. Try it. That's not bad. You have to turn your wrist a little more. That's better. Be quiet, John, I didn't touch her serious."

Jasper said to her earnestly, "Why'd you come away from the house with this yahoo? He's dangerous for a woman to be with alone that way. It's gettin' dark, and he grows hair on his hands after dark and his teeth get pointy."

Margot looked at John. "How soon?"

And the two men laughed fit to bust theirselves.

Seven

———

John didn't appear in any hurry. The night drew in over the line camp. The men lolled around and laughed and talked for Margot's attention. They told outrageous stories, but none was vulgar. They did try sly innuendos, but John wouldn't allow that.

The two laughed so much as they talked that Margot tried to figure out what all they were really saying, or almost saying, to her that amused them so much. Although they used the same words, men speak them with different meanings. They see incidents differently. They are another race entirely.

John was attentive to Margot and patient with the two men, and he was amused. He mostly listened.

John just shook his head when the two suggested he run along and they'd take care of Miss Pulver, personally. It'd be a chore, but they were gentlemen and they'd endure.

So they knew who she was. How?

When it was full dark, John rose and stretched. Jasper excused himself and left the cabin. John said to Margot, "You might want to refresh yourself?"

"Where?"

Ned explained, "We have a privy. Jasper's tidying it a bit."

The fact that a privy had to be tidied was not a plus. She hesitated.

Ned was earnest. He was so earnest that his eye wrinkles were white. He said, "He's washed it down. Just don't slip on the ice."

The two were such jokesters that she wasn't sure of anything they said.

John escorted her. The place was pristine. There was a spotless lavatory with running water.

When she emerged from the privy, she found John waiting for her. The two hosts had saddled their horses and had them ready.

Margot shook hands with both men and thanked them for their hospitality.

They said earnestly, "Any time. We'll be here a week. You'd be a nice change of pace. We'd like to discuss...what else people eat besides beans." And then they added, "You could open whole new horizons for us."

John said, "Let up."

So the two men stood back and avidly watched as Margot mounted her horse. They didn't watch John. And they stood watching after the two.

John stopped and looked back; then he waved his hand down once, telling them to go back inside.

"Why did you do that?"

"They think I'm taking you out in the bushes and they're trying to see which way we'll go."

She gasped, "What?"

"They have a lot of idle time. And, Margot, you need to know, if you'd been there alone, those two would have been helpful, careful and tongue-tied. They don't get to talk to too many ladies."

It was only then that Margot actually realized what kind of a man John Brown really was. That she had been attracted to him was true, but it was to him. This chance encounter with the men in the line shack had shown Margot exactly how John was. Tolerant, intelligent, a man.

She considered how he'd been with Jasper and Ned. And she had to smile. They were rascals, but he hadn't minded. The trick they'd pulled on the blocked door had been to tease John, but they hadn't made it impossible for him to get inside. They hadn't done anything to diminish him. They'd allowed him to win in her eyes. He'd kicked the door open and broken the blocking stick.

John hadn't been irked or flustered. He'd solved each problem as the two pranksters had gone along, and he'd kept them careful not to push too hard in teasing her. He'd been easy with the men. Just a look or a word from John had guided those two reprobates.

And John thought Lemon was the leader? The cohesive factor? She wondered. It would be interesting to see if it was so.

The rested horses were frisky and alert. They stretched their necks to see things and they blew and danced a little.

Margot rode well. She could handle the horse. John watched her. "You know, I do believe you could ride the pinto." The words were out before they could be stopped.

"Hah!"

"Now, Margot, you know I wouldn't put you into any danger. Lemon said you could. I objected. That's why Lemon said I should take you out and about and watch you. I find myself reluctantly agreeing, you probably could ride the pinto. You might even be able to tame him, too."

She slid a wicked glance over to John and about knocked him right off his horse. He said, "Don't do that."

"What?"

"Look at me that'a way. Not when I'm trying to control this stupid, birdbrained jackass."

"That darling?"

"I'll trade horses with you."

"All right."

"I was kidding!"

"You handle that horse superbly. If he is difficult and I can't cope, I won't be able to handle the pinto." She was logical.

"That could be true."

She dismounted, and so did he.

He held both horses while she mounted his.

The horse was a pussycat. "You lied." She gave John a glance.

"Now, Margot, you're going to accuse me of setting you up. Now you'll insist you can ride the pinto. Do you really know how to fall?"

"Like you, I was taught that first."

He rode without speaking, but he was agitated. She could see that.

He said, "Honey, I really don't want you to ride the pinto. I honest to God don't want you to. Lemon is all enthusiasm, and he thought this would convince me. It doesn't. I don't want you hurt."

"I understand. If you really are opposed to my riding the pinto, I will not."

So he, too, was given insight into another person. An important one, to him. She would not go against his wishes. It wasn't important for her to be challenged by something unimportant. She was secure without showing off.

Following on her horse, John watched her ride his, and he was emotionally touched by their exchange. That she would listen to his wishes was important to him. It showed she didn't feel the need to challenge anyone. She was secure.

He observed her sweet, feminine form as she moved, adjusting to the horse's movements along the trail. She turned her head and caught John monitoring her. She grinned and said, "Look, no hands! He knows the way home."

"Yeah. Be careful. It's dark and you can't see what might spook him."

"Okay."

"Want to change back?"

She said cheerily, "No need."

In him, love began crowding desire for equal attention. In two days? Yeah. Ever since she'd come so innocently into the library in that wicked dress.

They rode to the barn and there were some hands to take the horses. John thanked them. One man's response was mildly needling, "You're just lucky we're trying to impress the lady."

John speculated to the sky, "Maybe I can work a deal with her to ride with me every time."

Through the entire exchange, their voices were all so low that the sound did not carry to Margot, who was waiting for John at a distance.

Peanut was a huge man who loved peanuts but declined to be called Elephant or even Pachyderm. He scoffed. "If she had to ride with you—" his implication was that riding would not be on horseback "—she'd get tired of your slow pace, and we could replace you easy."

"Not likely."

Buck snorted and said to Peanut, "Sounds confident, don't he?"

"He's never had a finger on the pulse."

John said, "Careful now."

Buck sighed. "And he's picky."

Peanut asked, "What'a we get for wiping down your horses?"

"You get to keep your jobs."

Buck groused, "It's never any fun trying to bait sticklers. I've told you that, Peanut."

With his lashes covering his eyes, Peanut wondered, soft voiced, "Wonder if she'd like to be wiped down."

John turned his head to give Peanut a look, as Buck said, "No."

Peanut offered, "I could ask her."

This time it was John who said, "No."

The word was mild. Peanut looked back at John.

John said evenly, "The trouble with not being top dog is that no one pays enough attention to me. I'm a serious man. I don't tease." The gauntlet was down. They were not to make suggestive or improper comments about Margot in front of her... or to him.

Peanut's gaze measured John, and he smiled. "You're okay."

John said to Buck, "Thanks." For he knew if Peanut had gotten ugly, Buck would have tried to stop him.

John went to Margot and put his arm around her shoulders as they walked to the house.

He felt very protective. He was embarrassed that he'd been so rough on Peanut. He'd pushed the man. He should have just stayed quiet. Peanut was only being his ordinary rough self. But John couldn't allow the tiny nudgings at his possessiveness. So? He was possessive of her.

He squeezed her shoulder under his hand and looked down at her. She glanced up and smiled. He asked, "Are you tired?"

"No. You've forgotten how long I slept today. Wasn't it almost one this afternoon when I wakened?"

"I didn't think you ever would. I must'a been up those stairs forty times. I wanted to pull those covers back... and get in with you and waken you slowly."

Her steps faltered. "Don't talk like that. You make me forget how to walk."

He stopped as she walked on a step or two. She turned and looked back. His face was sober. She asked, "What's the matter?"

"I've just been struck by lightning. You."

She laughed in her throat, and her ears were surprised to hear the sound was very similar to that sort of male laughter. It was the female version.

He said in a husky voice, "I very badly need to be kissed."

"I smell like a horse."

"I smell like a studhorse."

"How unstrange."

"Unstrange?"

"Non?"

"That's 'no' in French. I badly need to be kissed. Think you could help me out?"

She glanced around carefully through the screening trees. Then she lifted her arms. Her riding gloves and the crop were still in her hands.

He put his arms around her and pulled her soft body against his. He turned his head so that his brim would knock off her Stetson, but his hat stayed on to block their faces. He curled his hips and pressed one of his hands down her back, molding her closer to him. His other hand braced the back of her head against the force of his kiss.

He was a little rough with his need to kiss her. To possess her. With his frustration, he found himself easing into tenderness and he smiled to himself. He was taking care of her, being careful of her. He loved her. How could he know that this soon?

He probably fell in love with her when she was tolerant of his being an alien. She was flexible.

He kissed her again. When he lifted his head, he told her, "You taste just right."

"So you ARE eating me. You sound so hungry."

"I love to feel you against me."

"You can't stand alone? You need support? You're idle and need something to do with your hands?"

"Yeah."

And she laughed that throat chuckle again.

He groaned against the side of her throat, "You have the wickedest soft laugh I've ever heard. You sound as if you like what I do to you."

"I do."

"Do you really? Or do you pretend?"

"I really do." Margot was aware it was the second time he'd referred to never being told he was wanted or that making love was nice. Who? Who had made him feel it was only he who was pleasured... Priscilla?

How could that be? Who else? If it wasn't Priscilla, wouldn't John's recent relationship with that woman have changed his memory of reluctant female participation?

He leaned his head back and studied her face. "What are you thinking?"

"How'd you know that?"

"You aren't concentrated on me. Are you all right?"

She rubbed her hands on his back under his jacket. "I was briefly distracted."

"Do I bore you, too?"

"Who bores me?"

"No. I'm the one who's boring."

She laughed. Her laughter bubbled. "You've said that before. It's nonsense. You are one of the most vital, interesting, in-control men I have ever personally known or witnessed. Most men are hollow. They have a talent in a field, but there are very rarely men who can go from their field and still be interesting. You are one of the few."

He was silent, staring at her. "Are you serious?"

"I never lie."

"How about bending the truth?"

"Not in these circumstances. You asked for my opinion."

"What if you thought I was a one-trick pony?"

"You wouldn't have asked. You know yourself. Someone has joggled your self-image and that's confused you. You were right to begin with. Your opinion of yourself is exact. You are not only humane, you are human. And you're multifaceted. Whoever told you otherwise is one dimensional and flawed. That person sees blindly, ten steps back through a pinhole."

"You think it's Lucilla."

"Why did you choose her name to fit the slot? Was it she?"

"I'm just curious if you're speaking from knowledge or jealousy."

She laughed. "So you realize I don't care for old Prissy Silly? You have to know that my older sisters have known her for a long time. She's some years older than you. She dumped you to try for someone bigger. Who? Maybe he can still be warned."

"I think you were right before, in saying it was Lemon."

"She is persevering. I doubt he'll have her. She'll be back. Then she'll look around and realize that you weren't so bad after all, and she'll try to mend her fences."

"Why do you say that?"

"She'll discover that your evaluation of yourself is honest and correct."

"You're good for my ego."

"That's something you lack."

"Your good?"

"An ego."

"Salty and Felicia said the same thing, but they're my parents. Parents have to be kind."

"No. Parents say the truth—but they say it gently. Instead of saying go ahead and climb the impossible mountain that has no top and isn't worth the foolish effort, they suggest building a dam or cleaning a river."

"How do you know all of those things?"

"I've watched my stupid, irritating, another-generation and out-of-step parents. They are insufferably right."

"Wait until you meet Salty and Felicia. You will go with me to Tweed's wedding?"

"I'd be delighted."

"You ought to realize that the family will assume I'm putting my mark on you."

"In what way?"

His voice was very gentle. "That I'm serious about you."

"Not yet."

"You'll let me know when it's okay for me to be serious?"

"You'll know."

"Margot—"

"I'll tell you when you can tell me."

"Are you going to be stultifyingly brilliant all of your life?"

"It comes in streaks."

He considered, looking off, then his glance came back to her. "I suppose I can handle that."

"That's the point of all this conversation—you can handle anything."

"No." He was serious. "There are some things that are beyond me."

"You are reluctant to harm other people's opinions of themselves, because you're vulnerable, too."

Holding her in his arms, he looked off into the night for a long while. It was then that she understood his saying she'd left him while still against him. Now it was he who, holding her, left her. She looked at his face and saw his distance. What did he contemplate so intensely?

He blinked. Then he tilted his head down and his eyes seemed to gleam in the dark shadow of his Stetson. "I want to hold you for the rest of my life."

"It would be awkward to do that for the next sixty years."

He smiled. "You find that you don't actually believe me, so you're sassy."

"Possibly."

He took a deep, freeing breath and smiled in such a wondrous way. He said, "By golly, I am starved. Woman, what are you doing dallying with me out here in the cold night when we could be eating?"

She reminded him, "I was leery of the hygiene at the shack. I've really only had a coffee-and-sandwich breakfast."

"Then I suppose it's time for our 'lunch.' Let's find out."

He picked up her hat, took her arm and walked with her to the door which he opened, watching her, and he followed her into the house.

He was different. She could feel it. What had occurred as he'd looked off into the night? His touch was different. It was possessive. He looked around differently. The two put their hats on two of the pegs in the back hall and hung their jackets below them.

They went up the stairs and separated to their own rooms to wash and change.

She chose a Texas winter wool in a tangerine color. It was a smooth, sleek, soft gown, and her shoes matched the dress color. She put her hair into a French roll, and her earrings were small pearls with three tiny strings of dangling pearls.

Her lipstick was the color of her dress. Her eyes were made up enough. And her scant perfume was a very light scent.

John was waiting for her in her hall in the attic. He was leaning back against the wall with his arms crossed on his chest. He had on a suit and tie, and he looked simply gorgeous—but different. He intimidated her just a little. He was a stranger. A confident stranger who sent tickles of thrills around inside her body in very odd places.

He smiled as he looked her over in obvious pleasure. "Mmm." It was a sound of pleasure.

She was inordinately pleased.

"Do you have your lipstick with you?"

"Yes." She indicated the small needlepoint bag.

He took a tissue from his pocket and dabbed at her mouth. "I want to kiss you."

She loved it. She took the tissue and wiped her mouth, then lifted her arms.

He just held her first. He groaned and squeezed her; then he kissed her. It was stunning. It was different.

He observed, "Do you realize we've known each other since last year?"

Her chuckle was intimate and wonderful.

"Would you wear this?" He held out a ring on his palm.

"What is this?"

"It's the only thing I have from my birth parents. Salty gave it to me when I was twenty-one. I'd like you to wear it."

It was a plain gold band, a little thicker than a wedding band. He had worn it on his little finger.

"You're rushing this. Even though we've known each other 'since last year,' you're on a rebound. I hesitate to make it awkward for you to get the ring back."

"If I want it back, I'll say, 'Margot, may I have my ring back?' "

"What if I said, 'No'?"

"Well, I'd get Buck and Peanut and Jasper and Ned and a couple of others, and we'd hassle you."

"I have five brothers."

"Wow. Under those circumstances, I'd marry you." She laughed.

He almost smiled. "Wear it." It wasn't quite a command. It was a positive nudge.

She took the ring from his palm and agreed. "Just for tonight."

"Okay. We'll go one day at a time. Wait. I get to put it on your finger."

She was then uncertain. Which finger?

"We'll start with this one." He lifted the index finger of her right hand. It fit. He grinned. "Ahh." It was a sound of total satisfaction.

He kissed her again. Then he kissed the ring, kept her hand in his, and they went down the stairs.

All the guests were there. Since it was a buffet, people could come and go at will. It was noisy and the laughter was nice. There were sassy debates and flirting women, and it was fun.

The three women who had been Margot's potential roommates were dispersed. Only one was left there and she was no longer a roomie... for Margot.

John leaned to whisper that information to Margot. He watched as she licked her pale lips with a darting tongue, and then he looked on down as her nipples peaked.

She would again be alone in that big, big room with all those beds.

Clint was there for supper. He cleaned up like a tidied highwayman, and he made a bold pirate's foray through the women. He paused for the first serious encounter as he really looked at an unaware Margot. John just watched Clint, who smiled and went on past with a marauding sailor's two-finger salute to John. John laughed softly.

Margot noted that laugh because the sound was different. It wasn't the woman-luring throat chuckle, it was a confident man's laugh. She asked, "What has pleased you that much?"

"I'm with you."

She noted with interest he hadn't said the possessive, She was with him. He'd said that he was with her. And yet the laugh was the King of the Mountain kind. That *was* what it was.

In a crowd that big, there was always a piano player. There were people who thought they were, and weren't, but there was always one who could play about anything. There was one there.

As he played, they sang the TV series songs, they sang the old songs of the sixties that their parents had taught them, and the men sang songs that were partly hummed.

Through it all was conversation and laughter and now and then a woman's mock indignant protest to male laughter. Some woman was being teased by a group of men. Which would she choose? Probably Clint.

Being a good host, Lemon was around and about. He was solitary by determination. And Margot wondered why he'd given that party. Why had he coaxed her into coming there? What had been his purpose?

She turned her glance to John and she was glad she had finally agreed to be there.

Lemon came along and stopped to talk to Margot. "You going to ride the pinto?"

"John says no."

"Ahh." Lemon considered her seriously with interest. "So that's how it is."

"As your financial adviser, he is concerned with your finances. He doesn't trust the horse and he's afraid you would be responsible for my poor, broken body."

Lemon glanced down at Margot's body, then looked over at John who watched him back.

They both smiled, just the interesting ghost smiles of men who understand each other. That made Margot frown. What did they understand?

Lemon moved away, mingled and chatted. John and Margot danced. At midnight they snacked and admired the diligent crew, which made the wondrous morsels appear and the debris vanish.

The marrieds were about the first group to fold. They made up the smallest segment. They drifted off, some of the women carrying their silly nothing high heels, walking stocking footed and sleepy, holding their husbands' hands.

It was Clint who whispered in a conspiratorial voice, "The chaperons are gone! Let's get down and dirty."

The rest laughed and went on doing what they'd been doing—singing, talking, dancing. Clint and the predicted woman eased away. Her low laughter could be heard in the hallway to the stairs.

There was some talk about going out and taking a midnight ride on horseback. No one made the move to start such an idea and get it going. They were all sleepy and lazy and ready for bed.

Lemon stayed around. John wondered if he was monitoring Margot. John could take care of her by himself. He didn't need anyone interested enough to check up on her.

Lemon understood John better than John ever knew.

By then, Margot was playing Chopsticks with the piano player, who was getting shaggy eared with his eyeteeth lengthening. So John said, "I have a piece I always play at parties."

The piano player wasn't interested, but Margot insisted. So John sat at the piano and he played "Good Night, Ladies," which John did brilliantly and with frills and trills. It was simply great.

And it closed the party. People drifted off. Margot sat at the piano with John and asked, "What else can you play?"

He simply looked at her and didn't reply. She blushed faintly, but she looked back. She said, "You're different."

"In what way?"

"I'm not sure."

"Is it good or bad?"

"You might take over from Lemon."

He chuffed a disbelieving laugh.

"I believe you're finally beginning to understand that you're a bigger man than you realized."

And he looked down at the piano keys and closed his mouth tightly so that his laughter didn't explode.

Margot sighed with great patience. "I don't believe we are always on the same level. I think your mind runs along under mine and makes all sorts of widening meanings to what I'm saying."

"That's close."

"Why were you so amused that you had to smother such instant laughter when I said you're more of a man than you think."

"You said I was bigger than I realized."

"Why is that amusing to you?"

He glanced over at her and considered. Then he lied. He said, "I saw myself as towering over this house."

"If you wanted to, you could."

"Which part of Margot's mushroom do I nibble?"

She knew about *Alice in Wonderland,* but she also knew that they were again talking on two levels. He knew both levels, but she was stuck on one. And she wondered if she would ever understand men. Margot decided John was worth the effort it would take.

Eight

———

John and Margot were just about the last to leave the ballroom. They wandered around the—by then—dimly lit lower floor, holding hands, reluctant for the night to be finished.

Lemon found them and strolled along, talking lazily. He'd shed his suit coat and walked with his hands backward in his back trouser pockets.

The three sat in a cozy alcove, overlooking the scrub mesquite. There was the moonless reflection of the snow, which had lasted the day, and it highlighted the black bare branches of the leafless mesquite trees and the circles of stacked cactus.

It was quite peaceful there, looking out, the men talking in a desultory way. With two long days passed, Margot was somewhat tired and lay back in her big chair, quite relaxed.

Lemon suggested, "Some cocoa would be nice." And he started to rise.

John stood up, saying, "Sit still. You've been hosting for forty-eight hours. I'll go."

"Call Chuck. He'll fetch it."

"Naw. The crew has been worked to a standstill. I want to tell them what a good job they've done."

So Lemon and Margot were left in the silence. Lemon studied the sleepy woman. "Glad you came?"

She said some "Mmms."

"Sleepy?"

"A little."

Lemon shifted lazily and put his ankle on the opposite knee. "You gonna ride the pinto?"

"No."

"How come?"

She glanced at Lemon. "John says not to."

"So. You minding him now?"

She shrugged. "He's logical."

"I think you could ride the pinto and make him behave. You're a good horsewoman."

"I've sure sat one for a long, long time."

"Did you ever show?"

"No. Papa thought that was a waste of good time."

"It's just competition. He could say that of any competition. Skiing or running or swimming."

"He thinks all those skills are a good idea, but to compete is irrational."

Lemon tasted the word, "Irrational."

"There are other things to do, too."

"A one-trick pony."

"Exactly. John and I were just talking about being one."

Lemon snorted. "You saying *John's* one?"

"No. I think he's a widely talented man. He's not a one-trick pony. I think Priscilla is."

"Ah, a little jealousy there?"

"Not jealousy, she's nothing to be jealous about, but—"

"I'm sure glad to hear that."

"Hostility, now, is another thing entirely."

And Lemon laughed.

But Margot wasn't amused. "She harmed his opinion of himself."

"He acts all right."

"I think he'll be all right. He's changed since last year."

Lemon was very amused. "Two days."

"People can change in seconds."

"Yeah. I've seen it happen. It was Chico. He was scared of being sent back to Mexico. He thought everyone was watching him. So I took him down to register. It was like dragging a cat into water. But after he'd registered and we walked out of the building, you should have seen him stand and just look around. It was wonderful."

"So is John."

"I thought it would be that way. Aren't you glad I convinced you to come here?"

"Why did you do it?"

"Because you two would be great together. And if I can get him settled down, he might stay."

"He would, anyway. He admires you."

"I work my tail off trying to give him challenges. He's so— So you won't ride the pinto?"

Margot glanced around and saw that John was approaching with a tray. He heard at least the last sentence and he said "No," as he passed out the steaming cocoa.

Lemon stirred his drink as he complained to John, "I don't see how you can interfere with my plots. I got this woman here so that I could coax her into doing SOMETHING about the damned horse. You forbid it, and she listens to you? How did you manage that?"

John was politely emphatic. "I don't want her hurt."

"She's tough as nails."

John gave Lemon a serious look. "She's a lady."

Lemon sighed impatiently. "The toughest iron women I've ever known have been ladies. They're just more subtle. And they always have low, soft voices. I never heard a one of them shriek or talk high-pitched. Even their shouts were low voiced, and very positive."

"Who was that?" Margot was curious, sure it was one of the women who'd gotten away from Lemon. She waited and tasted her cocoa.

"My mother. She's the most bullheaded woman I've ever met."

John suggested, "Let *her* at the pinto."

"Margot's bones'll heal quicker than Momma's." He sipped his cocoa.

Margot huffed, "You said the pinto would never pitch me."

Lemon licked the cocoa from around his lips before he said, "Well...he does go under low-hanging branches and through low sheds, and he'll roll if you don't watch him."

Margot guessed, "You're only mentioning those things now that you know I've promised John I won't ride the beast."

Lemon's eyelashes screened his amused eyes as he watched the swirling liquid in his cup. His voice was complaining as he stated, "Somebody ought to do something about that stud. He's prime for racing. I just can't get anybody to teach him basics."

Margot was logical. "Why don't you? You're a superb horseman."

"I don't have the time and, anyway, I'm a-scared of him."

Margot and John both laughed.

Lemon finished the last from his cup and told them, "It's true. I heard two mice scampering acrosst my bare floor and it sounded just like that pinto had gotten inside and was after me."

Margot said, "Aww."

John sighed hugely and said, "I'll see what I can do."

"No. I won't have you riding that bush stud. He smells you and thinks you're competition. It'll have to be a lady."

Margot put her cup into the saucer so quickly that it rattled, and she lifted an excited hand as she exclaimed, "Priscilla!"

Lemon dismissed that. "She's no lady."

An amused laugh puffed from John as he chided, "That wasn't gentlemanly." And he drank from his cup.

Lemon told Margot, "He's trying to make me act civilized."

John explained, "He was taken from his mother's care too early."

Lemon scoffed. "She was the one that threw me out!"

John asked, "Is there anyone who didn't understand that?"

Lemon groused, "No, even the juvenile judge agreed with her."

Margot questioned, "What on earth did you do?"

"Well—"

And John reminded Lemon, "She's a maiden lady and a guest."

"Oh, can't I talk sex to her?"

John's reply was brief, "No." He set his cup aside.

With the sound of his voice going up and down in exaggerated complaint, Lemon pointed out, "John, you've known Margot since last year. By now she's got to know the real us?"

"By actual count, that's two days. She doesn't look for flaws. She's not critical or fault finding—"

Margot snorted.

John's look pinned her as he pronounced, "A lady."

Lemon lolled back in his chair and argued, "Well, for all that, so's my momma. She's just testy, tempered and unreasonable."

John assured Lemon in a very kind voice, "You'd make a nun testy."

"One was. I had to go to the Catholic school once because the other schools wouldn't let me inside their hollowed doors an—"

John supplied gently, "It's spelled with an *A,* 'hallowed.'"

"Boy, these was hollowed because I fixed 'em that-a-way. It didn't take much. One was a pipe bomb, one was a Jeep and the other was Papa's new Ford. That was what finally ticked *him* off."

Margot inquired with real curiosity, "Why did you do all that?"

"I was opposed to formal education. But I've re-formed. I've gotten curious and I even . . . listen." But his conscience made him add, "On occasion."

John put in, "Rarely."

Lemon frowned at John. "Now, don't you say that. Remember two years ago when you told me to take along a bedroll? That the creek was rising? I did."

"You checked out the creek first."

Lemon tilted his head up and then down to his chest. "That is true. Mule Ears taught me those things when I was just a tad. It was the kind of learning I didn't mind tackling. It was words and figures . . . math figures, you understand . . . that thwarted me."

"Were you dyslexic?" Margot asked.

"Yep. But they didn't have all the help they have now for little kids. They just thought I was spoiled rotten and ornery. While that was true, I couldn't understand anything they were telling me. Everybody else could do all those things, and I couldn't understand why I couldn't."

She agreed. "That was tough."

"It made me understand nobody's perfect, and it made me face the fact—I wasn't perfect either."

Margot lifted her brows and asked, "So that's why you're so easy to get along with and pliant and humble?"

"Yep." He put his hands on his knees and slowly stood up to stretch and yawn. "You've outlasted me. I'm going to bed."

John groused, "What a lousy host."

Lemon sat back down.

"But don't let me delay you. You have our permission to vanish."

"Somehow I'm not surprised." He stood back up so effortlessly. He smiled down on the two attentive people who were of opposite gender and said, "Good night, chillen. Behave reasonably. If you can't do that, be as discreet as possible."

John said "Lemon," in a rather chiding way.

"I'm going, I'm going. Good night. It would have been a very dull party without you two here." He leaned over and kissed Margot's forehead. "Aren't you glad you came?"

"Okay. I'm glad. Now put down the gun."

Lemon expressed great surprise. "I forced you to say that? What sort of gues—"

John said, "Good night, Lemon."

Lemon put the back of his hand to his forehead and said, "I know when I'm not—"

"Lemon!" John put his hands into his hair as if desperate.

And the man laughed out loud, turned and walked away, still laughing. The sound was so amused that the two seated ones were forced to smile as they shook their heads.

"You're good friends." Margot observed the obvious.

"Most of the time." John got up and held out his hand. "I'll walk you up."

She considered John. "How do you know I'm ready to go to bed?" It was an inquiring statement.

"It's time."

"I suppose." She yawned. "See? You make the suggestion, and I respond."

"My name is Svengali. You're Trilby." He gave her his hand and helped her to stand.

"Who are they?"

"She sang like a crow. He was a hypnotist who made her sing like a lark."

"Ah-hah! You want me to sing!"

"Well, no. I just want you to do as I choose."

"Let me guess."

Holding her hand, he was leading her through the lower rooms to the stairway. There wasn't anyone else around that they could see. Some of the rooms were dimly lit, the rest were dark. Other than the faint tappings of her heels, there were no sounds. They could have been the only two around.

She stopped and braced her hand on his chest as she lifted her foot backward to take off one shoe and then the other. He took them from her. They looked small in his big hands. He again enclosed her small hand in his free one and led her up the stairs.

He was going to make love with her.

She knew that. She considered whether or not she would allow him to do it so soon. And she considered the reality of wanting him. She turned her head to smile up at him and share her amazing decision, but his face was serious, and his eyes on her were intent.

He was breathing through slightly parted lips, and he was looking down her body to her stocking-footed steps on the stairs. He noted the way her gown moved and adjusted to her movements, and he was very aware of her body beneath the gown. His hand squeezed hers and his fingers moved slightly to caress hers within his grasp.

He kissed her on the first landing to the second floor. He couldn't wait to kiss her. Her shoes were hard against her back as his hand pulled her close to him. His other hand was at the nape of her neck and those fingers supported her head against the hunger of his pressured kiss.

He slowly lifted his mouth from hers and there were myriad sounds in the stillness that betrayed the intimacy of his intense kiss. Intently, he looked down at her face.

They turned slowly and began to climb on up to the second floor. She whispered, "Priscilla taught you well."

If Margot had intended to cool him with a sassy comment, she was disappointed. Very quietly, he said, "Her name was Mary Jo, and it was in the second grade in Temple, Ohio."

Her whisper was sibilant. "Second graders kiss like *that?*"

He agreed almost silently, "They do in Temple, Ohio, if they're named Mary Jo."

She spoke softly, "Who did you kiss next?"

"Mary Jo rattled me, so I didn't kiss another girl until I was in the third grade."

She muttered, "Did you go from second grade to third grade in one day, as we did from last year to this one?"

He murmured, "Yeah."

Matching his hushed voice, she chided, "You're a very sudden man."

"I've been leading up to such a kiss ever since New Year's Eve when I saw you come into the library in 'that dress' and you locked the door."

She hissed, "There is nothing wrong with that dress!"

"Did I say there was?"

She murmured, "You keep referring to it as 'that dress,' as if it were a scandal!"

Almost aloud, he declared, "Well, it is!"

She chided softly, "Shh! And you've kissed me before now."

His voice low, he agreed. "I know, I know, but I can't get enough. I've tried to be considerate, but your mouth drives me almost as crazy as your body."

Faintly, she gasped. "Mary Jo's family had you deported to Texas?"

He agreed, "Salty and Felicia fought it and spent their entire fortune in the struggle, but I was deported. It's been a lonely life down here. There are too many men. Not enough women."

Still quiet, she guessed, "You've not been able to attract a woman?"

"Just Priscilla."

Soft voiced, she retorted, "That would tend to boggle any man."

As they started up to the attic rooms, they heard a woman's smothered laughter. A wicked sound. Margot watched the stairs. Peripherally, she saw that John turned his head and looked to see if she'd heard. She busily watched the stairs and heard the woman's wickedness echoed in John's low chuckle. He knew she'd heard.

She whispered, "Behave."

He gasped, "Now?"

Unfortunately, she breathed a chuckle that closely matched the woman's laughter. She explained in soft words, "It's a ghost. Didn't Lemon ever tell you about her?"

"No."

Very quietly, she suggested, "Well, you might ask him the next time you see him."

In low tones, John replied, "She's probably in his room. That's why he didn't invite a real woman here."

"I think the reason he didn't invite someone for himself was in case you would ignore me, and he'd have to act as host so I wouldn't feel like a fifth wheel."

The explanation struck John as the typical courtesy of Lemon. He would do something just that unselfish. Interesting. Or could Lemon have become interested in Margot?

They had reached the upper hall in the attic, and there wasn't a sound. Her door was open, the others were all closed. There was no one in her room. Again she had it to herself. A night-light was on and only on her bed the covers had been turned down.

John couldn't completely lick away his smile. He said, "I'll check under the beds." And he closed the door.

The tip of Margot's tongue quickly licked her own lips as she waited, her hands clasped in front of her.

He got down on a hand and one knee and looked under each bed. He found a man's sock. He looked in the closet and set her shoes on the floor. He glanced over her things, looking, and whistled softly over her red dress, hanging demurely limp on a hanger. He took it into his hand and wadded it up to show her how ineffective that small amount of material actually was.

In moderate tones, he asked, "Where's the slip you wore under this?"

"I didn't."

"You didn't have on a slip and you offered to take off the dress when you didn't have one ON? And I let you keep the dress on?" He was indignant.

"Even if you'd agreed, I wouldn't have taken off the dress, there, in front of you that way."

He came over to her. He put his big hands on either side of her face, and the heels of his hands turned her mouth up to his. He said, "You're out free and loose and there's no one guarding you? Isn't there supposed to be an escort for dangerous women so that men can be warned?"

She shook her head and her face was very serious.

He leaned his face to hers, his breathing was roughened and irregular. He put his arms around her and pulled her so close that any closer and they'd have been melded. She could feel his hard surfaces pressed against the helpless, unprotestingly eager softnesses of her body.

He made her feel odd, a bit faint, unable to breathe in enough and impossible to exhale enough. Becoming somewhat dizzy, she gasped as she tried to wiggle closer.

Having no conscience at all, that was when he kissed her the double-whammy woman-killer kiss. When she was willing mush, he asked her in a roughened, husky voice, "How about this dress? Will you offer to take it off?"

Her head wobbled around. He couldn't actually tell if she was indicating a yes or a no, so he bent down and lifted the hem and began to pull it up over her body.

She had to stop him and indicate the belt.

His hands trembled as he bent his head and tried to figure out the belt. She let him struggle with it as she watched him.

He glanced up at her face and had to kiss her again. He put his arms back around her and really kissed her. Then he had to help her stand so that he could concentrate on the belt.

He took off his shoes and kicked them out of the way. And he took off his tie and suit coat. He did those things without any trouble, but her belt baffled him. He took off his own belt easily enough, but he had a little trouble unzipping his trousers.

Then he pulled out his shirttail and took hold of the bottom. He told her, "Close your eyes."

She thought he might be modest, so she slitted them.

He simply ripped off the buttons as he pulled the shirt front open. He was very earnest, and he undid the cuffs and pulled off the shirt. He wore no undershirt.

Having watched how he opened his shirt, she had a clue and it sank into her befuddled mind. She stepped back and undid her own belt.

When he saw she could do that, he got out of his trousers.

But she stood there, still dressed, and not doing anything else about getting undressed.

He paused and considered. She hadn't objected. She had undone the belt. He went to her and kissed her another of those sinful, wicked, killer kisses, so that she was gasping and sort of pawing at him and making little sounds.

His hands were trembling, and he was uncertain, but he did prevail and he found the buttons on her chest that had to be undone. Having gotten that accomplished, he was distracted by the lace under the dress, covering her breasts. It was so feminine.

She was.

He became very slow and careful. He touched her softly, slowly. He really looked at her. His kisses then were sipping ones that were exquisitely thrilling to them both.

She was shivering with desire.

He asked, concerned, "Are you cold?"

She shook her head.

He considered. Then he smiled, hot eyed and potent. "You want me."

She nodded, serious, quick little nods.

"My God, woman, you're going to set me off. Here, let me take this beautiful dress off you before I tear it off."

And he did take it off very carefully.

She emerged from it and stood silently, wearing a lace-and-satin slip. And she looked so innocent. The contrast was stunning to John. His breathing was harsh and his whole body trembled. "Oh, honey—"

"Do you want to take off my stockings?"

"Yes." He replied so quickly that his word tromped on the last sound of her question.

She sat down on the edge of the bed, and he knelt in front of her. "I may go crazy." He stated that as a very real problem.

"Or I will."

His face lighted. It was the only way to describe it. It was as if a light turned back on inside him. He said, "You want me. You really *want* me!"

"Yes."

"Oh, Margot—" He put his head against her stomach, his arms around her hips, and just hugged her. It was very touching.

Margot put her hands into his hair and cupped his head. She soothed him as one does with anyone who is very emotional.

But her soothing was a balm on his feelings, and he rubbed his face slowly but hard against her stomach, and stretching up he nuzzled gently around her breasts. It was excessively erotic.

He sank back on his heels and looked at her. When he could calm himself enough, he lifted the bottom of that half-lace, half-satin slip and revealed the tops of her stockings. She wore a garter belt. He undid those in a careful way, with both hands, and that showed he'd probably never detached stockings from the fasteners of a garter belt—or he was unusually calculating.

He took hold of the stocking top and pulled it down. It folded over and came down over the rest of the stocking, so he had to go back and pull down the rest of it. He finally gathered it all at her ankle and pulled it from the toe. He asked, "Is that the way?"

And she smiled. "Yes."

He got cocky. He was already, but he began to act as if he had élan. He did the second stocking with as much concentration, but he was a little smoother.

Then he glanced at her face. He took her cold feet into his hot, hot hands and held them against his hot, hot body, warming her. And he looked at her.

He told her, "I want to put my hands on you so bad, but I'm scared to death I'll scare you."

She said, "Oh, good. If you can behave, then I can put my hands on you?"

Very earnestly, he said, "Oh, yes!"

But as she stood up from the bed in a slow motion, he took the bottom of her slip and, standing as she stood up, he brought it up and over her head...and off.

She had on lace panties that matched her lace slip. He stood dumb and silent, looking at her. He panted. It was as if he'd run miles and was staggering in toward his goal, at last.

She was restless. She moved. Having been so still, now she moved. She said breathlessly, "Sit down." And she moved aside, so that he could sit on the bed.

As he leaned over to sit down, his hands slid her panties down.

But her own hands were struggling with his briefs, and he had to help her. He did. He gasped, but he did help her. He said, "Careful."

A nervous wreck by then, he sat down on the bed. He put a hand to his head and his eyes were like an innocent's. He was mesmerized by her. He said, "Margot. My God, Margot."

Her panties were around her knees. She wiggled to get them to slide down her legs, and she kicked them off.

He shook his head very, very slowly from side to side, but he couldn't move his stare from her. He said in a very hoarse voice, "Margot, we've got to be careful. I'm not sure you can touch me. I'm really triggered."

"You want to make love to me."

"You noticed."

"Well, you're not subtle."

"If you'll let me make love to you now, I'll let you do anything you want to me afterward. I wish I could

let you have the freedom of my body—'' He breathed
for a while in a very erratic way and said, ''I can't even
talk about it.''

''Well, do you have a condom? I could put it on for
you.''

Rather quickly, he asked, ''You know how?''

''Well, no, but once a bunch of us got one and investigated how it worked. I believe I could roll it on for
you.''

''Not this time.'' He was very earnest.

''Well, let me watch.''

''I'm not sure I can handle even that.''

She smiled. ''You're very flattering to me.''

''I really want you.''

She shrugged. Her breasts moved with her shoulders' movement and she was breathtaking. ''I'm willing.''

''If we're very careful, I may be able to wait until
I'm in you.''

And she laughed softly. She laughed just like the
woman they'd heard downstairs on the second floor.

With some new insight, Margot told John, ''That
woman who laughed was making love with a man.''

''Yeah.''

Nine

Someone had put a heating strip down the middle of the bed. John said, "That was thoughtful. I was going to get in and warm the bed for you, and you know I'd lose my mind, with you on top of me, clawing at my body and shrieking like a scalded cat."

Margot replied snippily, "I never shriek."

"Now, you had to've slept in this bed last n—"

"It was warmed."

He smiled at her, his sun wrinkles deepening. "I'm glad it was warm." He looked down her. "I'd hate to have that body shivering." Then he considered. "Well, maybe a tad before I got you all hot and bothered."

She shivered a shimmer.

He gasped and rubbed his stomach while his sex went wild.

She was fascinated. "I hadn't known it could do that."

"It hadn't, either."

"Did you name it? My brothers all have names for...those."

He cleared his throat in a delaying manner as he sought a way to reply. "When we know each other better, I'll tell you...but on the promise you'll never tell anyone. Not *any*one."

"Does Priscilla know?"

"No. She never asked. She was never—curious about me."

Only then was Margot actually aware that the room was chilly. She hunched her shoulders and really shivered.

He took the pad from the bed and turned it off as he draped it over the chair close by. He held up the covers and said, "Quick."

She didn't have to ponder about getting into bed with him. She just scrambled in and hogged the warmed portion.

He took up his trousers and sought a condom. He took a steadying breath and concentrated as he carefully rolled it on.

He was so hot that he wasn't aware she was claiming the rights to the middle of the warmed bed as queen of the mountain. He sat down, lifted the blankets and swung his feet under them. He never paused. He pulled the covers up over his side as he continued his turn and ended up hovering over her.

She looked up, very big eyed in the soft night, with its snow-reflected light barely illuminating the room. She said, "You're letting in all the cold air."

So, of course, he crowded down on her, his heat radiating through her, his breath hot and scorching, his hands scalding her cool flesh.

His excited breath touched her cheeks as he said, "You're just lucky I was gentlemanly enough to come up here and help you sleep all cozy and warm."

"I could have had any number of the barn cats."

"They're wild."

"You're not?"

"Not entirely. But you're getting me that way pretty quick."

"I don't know what I should do. Tell me."

"I'll handle everything." He moved his hands on her. "I am so—taken—with you. I can't believe you would be willing. You're such a surprise. You're such a miracle. Do you really want me?"

That was the third or fourth time he'd said something similar. Why would he say anything like that? Why would he be surprised because a woman would want him? She said, "I have shivers down there, inside me, and I assume that's need. You excite me. I like having you kiss—mmm..."

So he had to show her that kissing was part of it all. And he showed her the variety that...well, he showed her a few, but he couldn't wait any longer. He moved her knees apart, and she helped. He ran his hands over her and made amazed sounds and relishing sounds. His hands moved just right, and she began to writhe and make her own sounds of gasps and murmurs.

He eased to her and said, "Easy, easy. Let me. It's okay. Mmm. You're so soft." But he couldn't tarry too long. And she helped him.

He tried to be slow and careful. She wiggled and strained and concentrated. He slid to the barricade and was temporarily stymied. He didn't want to hurt her.

He was breathing like a stud bull and he was sweating and slippery. He swallowed and gasped. So she took hold of him and forced the entry. His breath whooshed out as he made a guttural grunt and shivered, trying for control.

She gasped in amazement.

"Are you okay?"

"Oh, yes. Why... it fits. I knew it had to, but it has never seemed possible, and I've always wondered. But women said it was nice. And I just couldn't figure it out. But it is!"

He said hoarsely, "Hold still."

After a time, she mentioned, "You weigh more than I thought."

He said, "I'll move as soon as I'm sure I can handle it."

And after some more time had passed, she said, "I would like to move, I'm getting a crick in my neck."

"You can carefully move your neck, but don't push your chest up or move your bottom or your legs."

"How am I supposed to do that?"

"Just the neck." He added, "Be careful. I'm chancy."

She moved her neck somewhat. They were silent. He breathed and shivered. She said, "Are you going to sleep?"

He groaned, "Don't make me laugh."

"This is different than I thought it'd be. I like the feel of you on me and even in me, but there has to be more to it than this."

"I'm hair-triggered right now, and if either of us moves, I'll explode."

"Your whole body?"

"Sperm."

"I understand it's full of protein."

"And babies."

"It's a good thing you found the condom. Do you always carry one?"

"I got them when I went for the cocoa."

"How crafty you are."

"No. I'm doing something wrong because I should be able to make love with you and not just lie here balanced on my toes and trying for control."

"What if I do this?" She wiggled.

He gasped very fast, "Be careful!"

She hadn't realized how tense she'd been. She relaxed, which opened her more, and he sank in farther.

He groaned like a bull stuck in creek mud.

She slid her knees up alongside his hips and wiggled her chest under his confining body.

He lifted his head and said, "Margot, I'm so hot for you that I can't coax you along. I'm going to have to just go ahead, and I'm sorry. I would like this first time to be a dream coupling for you. It's going to be fantastic for me, but I'll make it up to you another time. May I?"

She shifted her shoulders in a limited shrug and said, "Sure."

He groaned yet again and lifted his head almost as if he were pained. Then he kissed her consumingly. And he moved. He swirled his hips and pressed into her—and he was gone!

In no time, he shuddered and collapsed on her. His breaths were harsh and sweat dripped from his hot body. He shivered with reaction. "Oh, Margot, I am sorry."

She chuckled low in her throat. "It wasn't at all disappointing. We just might do it again, now that you know how."

He choked a little with a feeble, surprised laugh. "You can't be this kind. Thank you, Princess. You are wonderful. I feel very beholden to you for tolerating me."

"Tolerating? I really liked it. I do know there's more to it than what we just did. But I'll wait for your revival and see what else happens."

He lifted himself on trembling arms and fell off alongside her with a groan.

She raised up on an elbow and put her hand on him to ask with some concern. "Are you all right?"

"I've just had the best that's ever happened, but I didn't take you along."

"Pooh, there will possibly be another time. If you aren't willing, Clint might be coaxed."

He growled, "Stay away from Clint. I'll handle you."

"Now?" She was laughing.

"Well, not right away."

She lay back, amused, charmed, needy. She looked over at his inert body and her smile was sweet, her eyes gentle. Think of the power of the sex drive. Think of the discipline people used for control. It was nice she could say she'd known him for two years. She had. And all that time, she'd known Priscilla was not the woman for him.

She had watched him and listened to people talk about him, and worried about him being in Priscilla's snare. He'd been zonked by that witch. And Margot had been given the chance to taste him. It was she who had locked the library door so that she—who wanted him—could be bold and seduce him. She was able to tease and tempt and be available.

He was in her bed, sated by her body and asleep in sexual satisfaction. Drained.

She was filled with want.

She was no stranger to wanting. Just about any healthy person felt the drive. But she turned to fit her body along his side. She turned off the single light, settled down to sleep, and her dreams were erotic. That was no surprise.

John wakened. It was dark. He wasn't alone. Along his side he could feel the distinctive, different, soft body of a woman. Margot. She hadn't made him leave, and she hadn't left him! His reaction was electric.

But... different than she expected. He was apologetic. "Sorry I fell asleep."

He felt...awkward? She replied, "I was tired, too."

"I mean I'm sorry I didn't go back to my room."

"I doubt anyone would have noticed where you slept."

"I meant I'm sorry I conked out on you and didn't leave."

"Why would you do that?"

"You don't mind that I slept here?"

"No, I liked you here next to me. You're like an oven. Didn't you want to be my furnace?"

"I love it. I liked waking and finding you here. It was a dream."

"It can't be much of a dream. You slept with Priscilla."

"No. We never shared sleeping together. She didn't—"

"I don't want to know your intimate habits with—her. I'm jealous."

He slid one hand under her shoulders, and with his other hand he scooped her closer, arranging her head on his shoulder and her body along his. "Margot, you are too different from her for you to be jealous of her. She isn't any competition for you. You're magic and mud pies and sass and flirting and sparks and innocence."

"Innocence? How could that be?"

"I haven't changed you...yet."

"Yes, you have."

"Because of a brief invasion? Yes. In that, you are altered. You know, now, I'll fit." His voice was very tender. "But I haven't made love to you. May I, now?"

"That sounds like you're trying to seat me in an auditorium."

"Are you being snippy?"

"I'm not sure."

His chuckle was exquisitely intimate, it was so low and soft. It was so tender.

She put her hand up to his hair and combed it from his forehead with her fingers.

That position opened her body to him and raised her mouth just right. He kissed her. And she melted.

She murmured and moved in little squirms. She gasped between his kisses, and she inflamed him.

He seemed cautious and hesitant. She encouraged him. She put her knee up over his hip a little way which was shockingly bold for her to do.

He hugged her and said, "I have to clean up a little. I'll be right back." He released her, got out of bed and went to the bathroom down the hall.

Margot lay there, agitated and wondered if all seductions were as frustrating. She was tempted to get out of bed and hide somewhere just to see if he was interested enough to search for her.

But then she considered that was adolescent. Also he'd never slept in Priscilla's bed. How curious. Maybe he flung his arms around or snored thunderously?

She considered the lights and shadows in the big room as she lay there restless and somewhat impatient. This wasn't what she'd anticipated as her phenomenal, magical, reaching-the-stars First Time.

She heard the bathroom door open and she was still. He came quietly into the shadowed room and silently closed the door. He came to the side of the bed and hesitated. It was only then that she realized he felt a petitioner. A beggar. John?

She lifted the covers and heard his breath intake. He was surprised she'd welcomed him?

He eased carefully into bed like a dog who knows he isn't supposed to be on the couch. He tried to minimize himself.

She was appalled at the very idea and was sure she must be mistaken. She said, "I wasn't sure you would come back."

"Oh, Margot—" He just whispered the words.

She put her hand to swirl the hair on his chest. "I can't believe you could go out into the hall naked and come back to bed still warm. You must have a body furnace that is—"

"I thought you might have locked the door."

"Now, why would I do that, when I intend to seduce you?"

"You . . . what?"

"Well, I've let you have a little nap and I ought to be able to coax you into enough interest that we can—"

"You really want me?"

"What does it take to convince you? Are you that dense?"

"I just can't belie—"

And she'd kissed him.

He was surprised. His mouth clamped on hers, and he breathed harshly through his nose. His arms closed around her cautiously, to see if she would allow it; and when there was no objection from her, he pulled her to him and got serious.

She unstuck her mouth from his and whispered, "Slow down."

"I can't believe you'd let me—"

And she growled in a wicked purr, "I'm not *letting* you do anything. I'm having my wicked way with you. Now that I'm experienced, I know how this caper works."

And he laughed in chuffs. He didn't release her or move. He just turned his head aside and laughed almost helplessly, trying not to make any sound.

She sighed gustily and was positive. "I can. Don't for one minute think that I can't handle you. I'll roll on the condom first."

"I already did."

"That was thoughtful. A good attitude. Brace yourself, I'm going to get familiar."

"A voracious woman?"

"I'm not sure. Just relax and don't interrupt."

"I've gone to heaven?" he asked.

"No, you're in my bed."

"That's close enough."

With his words, she asked, "What do you mean? You don't want me to—"

"Your bed is close enough to heaven," he explained.

"Your thinking is limited. You'd better wait until you say that, this could be a nightmare for you. I'm not at all skilled."

"I'm tolerant. Go ahead. Do your darnedest." He spread himself out. Then he said, "Don't take too long."

"That was the way it was last time—for you. This time is for me, and we're going to do it my way. Don't get excited."

"You can't have any idea how you affect me."

She put her hand on him and waggled him. "Oh, yes. Either I did that or you're just easy. Whichever way it is, you're susceptible and you're in my power. Behave."

"Isn't being in your power and behaving in these circumstances counterproductive?"

"Don't go logical, feel."

He drew in a breath. "Why, Margot Pulver!"

"Mmm."

She did all sorts of things to him—to attract his attention. She had him trembling and panting. And she allowed him the freedom of her body.

He groaned, "Honey, you're driving me right up the wall."

As she moved her shoulders salaciously, she murmured, "How could you say that when I'm on top of you?"

Puffing, his voice shaking, he told her, "I have limits. You either have to give me a few minutes to settle down, or I'm going to go off like a skyrocket."

She swallowed with some difficulty and slithered on him. She managed to tell him in whispers that were wicked, "I'd like to see that sometime. But right now I think we can go ahead ... I feel as if ..."

He turned her over, and they panted and shivered with their need. She was pawing at him and moving in sexual slithers, and he just took over and set them both off. It was spectacular.

The skyrocket probably carried them far beyond the earth. They apparently hung in suspension, tightly holding on, and the burst was remarkable. They saw colors and their senses danced and writhed in erotic savorings. They hung in space for an endless, euphoric moment before they began to slide slowly back to earth.

They lay inert, mostly just working at breathing and trying vaguely to figure out where they were. She said, "Wow," a couple of breathless, whispering times. And he patted her shoulder in a floppy way.

They were groggy. He finally managed to turn his head enough to look down at her pale face, and he asked carefully, "Who are you?"

"Margot Pulver."

"How can you remember that at a time like this?" He was a little indignant.

She said, "Wel-l—"

And he said, "Shh."

It took him a while to recover. He lay and breathed and patted her shoulder a couple of times in a comforting way. He didn't say or do anything else for some time. Then he moved and released her from his weight before he raised up on his elbows and peered into her face.

He asked seriously, "Are you all right?"

Her eyes were closed, her face was so pale, but she smiled and said a whole lot of *mmm*'s.

Still trembling, he told her earnestly, "You're a miracle." And he told her, "I can't believe you're real. Are you a dream?"

"Should I pinch you or bite you?" She sleepily gave him a choice.

"You can do anything you want to me."

In a sleepy voice, she murmured, "I believe I'll keep you."

And his eyes filled with tears.

When they wakened in the morning, the sun was out and they could hear the drip of the melting snow. In Texas, the only reason to have gutters on houses was to catch the scant rain for the cistern. That didn't include the flooding rains of 1992 when cisterns overflowed and there was more water in Texas than anyone alive—there—had ever seen.

He watched her, his face cautious. He wasn't sure how she wanted to be treated on this morning after.

She grinned and said, "Good morning, lover. You ought to be bottled for lonesome women."

He shook his head several times and said emphatically, "This sort of thing has to be done personally, you know that. And I'm not available for any other woman because, if you will recall that simple fact—how's that for TEXAN?—you said you're keeping me."

"Of course."

"My breath isn't too bad mornings, how's yours?"

"Okay, I think."

"I wouldn't care if you smelled like a homeless dog, I need a kiss. Would that be okay with you?"

"We could try a cautious, friendly one."

They kissed gently. He was careful of her. He hugged her very gently. "You smell so nice."

"So do you. You smell different and interesting, and I like it."

They smiled at each other. She appeared contented to be held, and he sure did want to hold her.

However, to distract himself from what else he wanted, he mentioned the filled cisterns and said, "We're dreading the hoof rot and the overgrowth and the foundered cattle who eat too much fresh growth. It ferments in their stomachs and causes bloat."

She said insincerely, "How fascinating." Then she was logical, "With meat in such disrepute, I'm surprised you all are still raising beef."

"Our beef's lean and mean. We raise it for the men in this country who sometimes remember they need a good steak."

"Raw, of course."

"Pretty near."

She laughed and rumpled his hair. She had her face up so that she could look at him. So he cautiously kissed her, savoring it and the feel of her naked body so innocently against his woman-sensitive one.

She said, "I can't remember when I've slept with anyone. Not even at scout camp. I like this. Would you mind sleeping up here?"

"Let's move down to my room."

"Oh, no." She shook her head. "We can't do that. I can't carry my stuff down to your room! I'd look like a scarlet woman."

He thought about that. "You asked me to move up here."

"No, I didn't. I asked you to *sleep* up here. Discreetly."

"How do I do it...discreetly?"

"You don't move all your clothes up here. You watch until the coast is clear, then you sneak into my room, quietly close the door and slip into my bed, and do the reverse of that in the morning. Simple."

"Do I look like that kind of man?"

She hesitated and then said slowly, doubtfully, "Why...yes."

"I am."

And she laughed in a very softly sexy, intimate way.

Her laughter was balm to his ears and ego. He asked, "Would you like breakfast in bed?"

"No. Better not. Everyone would think I was sick and avoid me."

"We could pretend you are and be quarantined together."

"Now, now, don't you tempt me."

He asked with instant earnestness, "Would you be tempted—to just be with me?"

"You hadn't noticed that I locked the library door in order to trap you?"

He said, "I thought you wanted to be alone."

"No. I'd watched. I had a condom with me. I was going to get you."

He stared.

"I've shocked you?"

He replied, "I wish I'd waited."

"I kissed you and you immediately suggested we join the others."

"I was trying to protect you."

"From gossip?"

"From...me."

She sighed impatiently. "You could have asked if I wanted to be protected—that way."

"I can't believe I've found you."

"I've been hanging around for almost two real years, waiting for you to notice me."

Without questioning, he wondered, "How could I have been so blind?"

"Priscilla. I do have to admit that she is something to see."

"She isn't you," John was sure.

"I'm not sure how you mean that, but I—"

"You are a long way past what she is. I had no idea there was any woman like you."

Margot asked, "Who's willing?"

"You like me. You want me."

Margot pulled back to frown at John. "You've said that before. What did you have to do, rape her?"

"No, but I was the...supplicant. She allowed it. She didn't—" He bit his lip. "A gentleman never tells a lady about another woman."

"She sounds so...unwilling. What drew you to her?"

He shrugged slightly and moved his lower lip up a little. "She's a lot like you."

Indignant, offended, Margot asked, "WHAT?"

He looked at Margot a little startled and replied, "She's independent and strong."

"Priscilla?"

"Yes. She lives and does exactly as she chooses."

"And occasionally as you choose?"

"Chose. We've been separated since last spring."

"You make the 'separated' sound as if you'd been married."

"I wanted to get married. She wouldn't."

"Are you terribly hurt by her?"

"I thought so. But then you came into the library and distracted me."

"Well, you were fascinating. I'd never met a man before who was harboring an alien."

"You were a handful."

"For a grieving man, you were lecherous."

"That dress—"

"Don't you DARE say one more word about that dress!"

"Why are you so hostile about that dress? Other than the fact—now hear me out—other than the fact that it is a scandal and it caught my attention, there's nothing wrong with it."

"You always say THAT DRESS and not 'your dress' or 'that gown,' but THAT DRESS!"

"I'll try to watch my tongue."

"How're you going to do that?"

He tried. He stuck out his tongue and tried to see it, looking cross-eyed.

"You can look cross-eyed!"

"Can't you? Everyone normal can."

She said a small, "Oh."

"You can't?"

"I've tried so hard. It isn't possible. I figure I'm further along in the mutation of the human species."

He laughed. "You would be a woman who could take a flaw and claim it's an advancement in civilization."

"It has to be. Almost everyone can cross their eyes."

"You don't consider yourself as a throwback?"

"No."

He laughed out loud. Then he caught her leaving the bed and he hauled her back and said, "With special injections, you may be brought up to the present mutant level."

"Let me guess, the injec—"

"Right."

"I didn't finish my question."

"With the urgent need to save you, it is imperative to start the injections immediately. We can't waste time in this."

"How kind."

So they were a little late to breakfast. Everyone else was gone from the table, and only two place settings remained.

John went to the sideboard and lifted lids naming what was left. Fred came in and asked, "Breakfast food or lunch food?"

John said, "Any food."

Margot said, "Breakfast."

"Be right back. Coffee there in the pot. Tea's in that pot. Orange juice in the yellow pitcher."

John poured them each a glass, and they sat down.

Fred came back with a tray on which sausages and bacon and eggs were piled on two plates. The stack of toast would have fed the whole Pulver family for breakfast.

Margot said, "I'll just have tea and toast." Then she watched John eating and decided she could handle an egg from her plate. Then she ate a sausage from her fingers. She put some apricot jam on her toast. She had another egg. More tea. Another piece of toast.

Lemon came in and stood looking at them fondly. He sat down and poured himself a cup of coffee. "You children all right?"

John chewed and licked his lips. His voice was ordinary. "Yeah." And he gave Lemon a level look.

Lemon said, "We have a surprise guest."

John was using a piece of toast to help his fork with an egg-yolk-coated piece of bacon. Something in Lemon's quiet voice made John glance up. Lemon's eyes were serious. John asked quietly, "Who?"

"Lucilla."

Ten

John patted his lips with his napkin as he rose. He lay the napkin by his plate and said, "Excuse me, Margot." Then he asked Lemon, "Where is she?"

"In the morning room." Lemon considered John very seriously. His eyes were steady, his head slightly tilted.

And John left the room.

Margot sat, stunned. She lifted her eyes to meet Lemon's studying gaze.

He observed her soberly.

She pressed her napkin against her mouth rather firmly, then lay it aside. She said, "I believe I shall ride the pinto."

"There's no need."

"I wasn't asking your permission. I shall ride the pinto. Will you please see to it that he's saddled?"

Margot was treating him as a lackey, or like someone who'd harmed her deliberately. He said softly, "She was not invited. She simply arrived."

"When?"

"Last night. She came to see John, but he wasn't in his room."

With firm control, Margot looked straight at Lemon and said with dismissal, "He was probably out at one of the line shacks."

Lemon lifted his head and allowed his chin to sink down to his chest as if he agreed, but he was only acknowledging her comment.

Having dismissed John from her life, she then dismissed Lemon from the room. She told him, "See to it that the pinto is saddled. I shall change into my gear."

He rose as she did and he said "Yes, ma'am," as if he were being polite.

She gave him a shriveling glance as she passed him and walked on toward the stairway.

She was annoyed to find that Lemon caught up and was pacing her. He said, "John didn't invite her here."

"He ran to her at the first chance."

"He is a gentleman. He is an old acquaintance. He would have to know if she was searching for help."

"There are telephones."

"She had called his place, and there was only the answering machine. She came by here to see if I knew where he was."

Margot gave Lemon a killing look. "So you said he was here."

"'Somewhere around' were the words I used."

Margot stopped walking and faced Lemon, who had taken another step. Stopped, Lemon turned his head, and then turned his body some, in order to look at Margot. He was serious.

She asked intensely, "Why couldn't you have said that he wasn't here?"

Lemon's reply was gentle. "She would have found him sometime. It's better to face her now."

"Later, John could have had a stronger feeling for me."

"Or maybe not."

"Go see to the pinto." She turned away toward the stairs.

"Margot." He stopped her by taking her forearm briefly in his hand. "I had no choice. John's car was out there in the parking area. If I'd lied, she *still* would have found him."

"She used him."

"Everyone knew that—except John."

"That witch!"

"True. But there are other sides to Lucilla."

"Hah!"

"Keep an open mind."

"I've loved John for almost two years."

"You had a crush on him. He was unobtainable. Your crush was for a dream man."

"He is one."

"In just this time?"

"All along." She was positive. "He's the man I want."

"What if she's the woman he wants?"

She refused the large tears that welled in her eyes and she forbade their spilling over. "I'll change."

"Are you sure?"

"Yes!"

"Margot, if that horse pitches you and you break your neck, John would break mine."

"That's your problem."

He frowned at her and complained, "You always seemed such a pliant child."

"I'm a woman."

"I had noticed. If John's stupid enough to go back with Lucilla, how about giving me a chance?"

"No."

"You're just like your sisters."

She went on off, with quick steps, and went up the stairs.

Lemon stood in the lower hall and watched her out of sight. Then he smiled slightly with some bitterness before he went out to tell Peanut to saddle the pinto.

Lemon was watching as Peanut walked the damned pinto up and down the stable yard. Even Peanut wouldn't voluntarily ride the beast. But the pinto was alert and looking around and shaking his head to indicate to Peanut that he'd prefer to be freed.

Ham-handed, Peanut didn't allow the horse to do much of anything. And Lemon watched. He didn't want the horse too frisky before Margot got on the beast, so Peanut was walking him and getting some of the steam out of him.

Margot came out of the house, wearing a Stetson with the string guard up under her chin. She was dressed in denims with a sweater under her jacket and she wore boots. She was pulling on gloves.

The snow was melting by then and the sandy ground was soaking in the moisture. There were still unmelted banks of the snow in the piles against barriers like the fencerows or the corrals and in the shade of the house and the outbuildings.

The wind was gentle and just right, cool enough but warming. And the day was glorious.

Businesslike, Margot stood and waited for Peanut to bring the horse to her. That conduct was a clue to Margot. She expected courtesy and she got it. In turn, she was courteous, considerate and compassionate. The three big Cs that are jammed down a lady's throat forever.

Right then, she felt none of those things. She looked the pinto in the eye and reached to take the reins from Peanut.

Peanut didn't give her the reins. He held the horse steady while she mounted; then he handed her the reins.

She gave him a glance that was aloof, and she said, "Thank you."

"How's the cinch?"

She moved. "I believe you've done it perfectly."

Peanut betrayed himself. He said, "Be careful."

She nodded once to acknowledge he'd spoken and replied, "Stand aside."

And Peanut helplessly stepped back.

There is something about a determined woman that even horses recognize. The pinto went through his paces and did as he was directed. He was chipper and flamboyant and he enjoyed himself. She didn't let him get away with anything.

She took him over toward a shorter fence and was circling to approach it when John met them head-on. He reached out and took hold of the reins just under the chin of the pinto, just exactly as if the pinto were an ordinary horse, and he stopped the pinto cold. The pinto—and Margot.

The horse tried to shake his head, and John wouldn't even allow that. He was watching Margot. He said softly, but so that the avid watchers could hear, "You really know horses."

But John's face was stern. He did a very excellent job of concealing his fury with Margot. He didn't fool her.

She looked at him coldly. She said, "Release him. We're going over the fence."

"Allow me."

"I choose to do this."

With his words spaced out exactly, he said very, very quietly, through his teeth and just to her, "Over my dead body."

She looked down her nose at him and replied through stiff lips, "Very likely."

The horse tried to pull his head away. John flicked a look into the horse's eye and said "No," in a quiet voice. Then he looked up and appeared to smile kindly, but his eyes were deadly. He said to Margot, "Get down."

There was no way she could refuse. Not without making a fool of herself... or of John. She chose to get down.

He took hold of her arm and said, "I could wring your neck. We'll talk about this later."

She said with a courteous-looking hiss, "Perhaps." And she smiled gently as she turned and walked off.

But inside the house, she stood back from a window and watched with her heart in her mouth.

John got up on the pinto and put him through his paces again. And the pinto fought the entire way. John was kind and gentle and talked to the horse. But the horse didn't want to do those things, and John wouldn't use a riding crop.

Then a strange woman came from another door into the area. She wore a formal riding outfit and she was simply beautiful. Margot, of course, recognized her immediately. It was Lucilla.

She went over to the struggling pair, the horse and rider, and she reached over to the horse's nose as John told her something in a stern manner.

She lifted her chin, took hold of the reins just under the horse's chin and gave John a head toss of dismissal.

John refused.

Lemon came into view. Guests were such a nuisance. He sauntered over, his hands backward in his back pockets, and he reasoned with John.

John listened. Lucilla talked to the horse, who loved it. And Lemon didn't gesture. Gestures were annoying to the pinto.

Lucilla explained something and gestured. The pinto didn't mind Lucilla gesturing.

And watching, Margot understood that while Lucilla could mesmerize men, she also enchanted studhorses. It was a bitter pill to swallow.

Margot went up to the attic room and began to pack.

John came up and stood in the doorway. Faintly, Margot could hear men cheering outside where the jumping fences were. She knew Lucilla had managed to get the damned horse over the fence—and more than likely was taking him through the course quite successfully.

Margot gave John a cool glance and went on with her packing.

He asked, "Where the hell do you think you're going?"

"Away."

"Not . . . home?"

"Not right away."

"Then where?"

"I'll leave a forwarding address."

She turned away, and he lost his temper. He took four or five giant steps into the room. He took hold of her upper arms in a firm grasp, and he shook her once. Their faces were red, and their breathing was high, and they were simply furious!

She said in a very controlled voice, "How dare you!"

"How dare *you?* What the hell's the matter with you? Why did you go hightailing it out there and get on the pinto when I told you, loud and clear, you were not to ride that animal and you agreed! What in hell made you decide to do a harebrained thing like that?"

"Let go of me!"

He did so, but he stayed looming over her. "Tell me this minute!"

"You have no idea?"

"If I had any inkling at all, I wouldn't have come up here to hear what possible excuse you can give. Now you just settle down and tell me what sort of bee's in your bonnet. And believe me, Margot, it had better be good."

"I don't have to tell you anything. I'm a free person. I'm over twenty-one, and I can do as I damned well please. Back off!"

The word was quiet. "No."

She blinked. He now appeared quite calm. He watched her with avid eyes and he was very serious, but he was no longer angry. Think of the control of a man who could manage that. She was impressed.

She, on the other hand, was still furious. At him. She gave him a scathing glance and shut her mouth. She took up her packing again.

"Has someone called you away?"

Could he be that dense? "No."

"Then why are you so mad and why are you packing to leave?"

She felt no need to instruct him.

"Has someone offended you?"

Yeah. Guess who. She went on silently packing.

"If you will tell me what's the matter, I'll fix it."

"You already have."

"I already have...what?" He encouraged her to elaborate.

"Fixed it. Us. Life. The pinto. And *Priscilla!*" She slammed her last garment into the case and zipped it with great familiarity—and there was her lace-and-satin slip, not packed.

"What does Priscilla have to do with you riding the pinto and now packing?"

She looked at him. Was it possible he didn't understand? She considered him very seriously. "Why are you up here when Priscilla is down there riding the pinto?"

"Because you disappeared and I have to know why you'd risk your damned neck on that horse when I made it clear you were not to ride it...and you agreed...at that time. What changed your mind?"

"You got up from the table and ran to Priscilla the very instant you heard her name."

"I excused myself to you."

"And ran to Priscilla!"

He stared at her. "Margot? Are you . . . jealous?" His voice had turned so gentle.

She moved minutely in eight hundred different ways, trying to deny it, but she was unable to say anything else, "Yes. Horribly!" She glared at him and burst into tears. How humiliating.

"Oh, honey, how could you possibly be jealous?" He went to her and tried to take her into his arms.

The kindness unwomaned her. She turned her back and wept into her folded slip, knowing her eyes and nose would be red and she'd look ghastly. He was a gentleman. He was trying to be kind to a reject and let her off lightly. He'd take one look at her mottled, soggy face and he would be revolted.

He gave her his clean, big handkerchief and said, "Aw, honey, don't cry."

She took the handkerchief and went over to the window. She sat on the center cushion of the sofa that faced the windows and the view from three stories up. It was spectacular. She had never noticed it. Not in three days' time. She didn't then, either.

There were sounds in back of her. He was doing something. He was busy. She turned and glared over her shoulder. It was probably her red nose that made the whole side of the room light up.

Quite easily, she saw he was . . . unpacking her clothes and putting them away. And he held "That Dress" in his hands before he hung it carefully in her closet. He then picked up her suitcase and carrying case and put them into the top of the closet.

She turned around before he could catch her watching and know she knew he'd unpacked her things.

He came across the room and around the end of the sofa. He simply sat on one side of her, crowding her in an embarrassing manner. She didn't know of any reason to move aside, give him room and be welcoming to him, so she didn't budge from her space. She snubbed him.

He put his arm around her shoulders along the back of the sofa and just about enclosed her. She moved her shoulders in a good twitch to let him know she knew what he was doing and she did not approve.

In the nicest, most tender voice ever, he asked, "Are you going to forgive me for being kind to an old acquaintance?"

"Not right away."

"There are times when I'm unreasonable, too."

"Are you implying that I'm being unreasonable?" She was indignant.

"No. I just didn't want you to believe for one minute that I'm perfect."

She snorted.

"I didn't know a lady could snort so delicately. You are a wonder!"

So was he. He was making it so easy for her to get down off another kind of high horse. She'd never given him one chance to explain or for her to understand. She'd just gone off in a snit.

Next to her a measured voice said, "I have regained control. You are to explain s-e-x to me. We need this information."

She turned her blotchy red-nosed face his way and asked, "Now?"

"You are more attractive than any of the other human creatures on this planet of your gender."

"Good grief."

"What is grief that it can become good? In the male manual it claims that grief is—"

"You idiot!"

"How do you spell 'idiot' exactly? Wait. I have found it. It means 'A person exhibiting mental deficiency in its most severe form and requiring constant care.'" He pleaded, "Care for me. Teach me *s-e-x*. I understand it is the most calming application for the human male, and this male's body is very unsettled."

"John—"

"John is a place to relieve oneself."

"Stop!"

"Cease progress."

So she kissed him. That surprised her, too.

John took over and crushed her to him, kissing her into a swoon. He picked her up and carried her to the bed. He dropped her on it, and she exclaimed.

He was surprised. "It says, 'Put her on the bed.' Did I not do it right? You are there."

"Gently."

"'Mild and amiable.' You did not bounce but two feet." As he spoke, John closed the door before he stripped off his clothing. "These coverings are complex and uncomfortable. Why did you change from going naked? Oh, yes, in Eden the Apple gave the feeling of shame."

He took off her clothes and compared their bodies. He was fascinated. He bragged that he had the appendage she lacked. He felt cheated that his nipples weren't like hers but were surrounded by hair. He tried hers and complained there was no milk. "Back to the manual."

He learned about *s-e-x*. He didn't believe the method of coupling. It wasn't logical.

He asked what sort of sounds he should make and how the movements should go. He was fascinated by the condom and blew one up, tied it and batted it across the room. He didn't believe it was for the appendage.

He was so convincing that she almost believed him. She asked, "Are you real?"

"I'm as real as anyone you've ever known. I love you, buttercup."

"My hair is brown."

He gently lifted strands of her hair. "Is this brown? I thought it was blond. I get the words confused. Learning such a strangely mixed-up language is difficult. Ours is more direct."

She did persevere, and they did couple in the manner she had indicated. It did work, it was pleasurable and felt good. It was wonderful! He made appreciating sounds and he was tender and gentle and savoring.

He did movements that were different and he did things she hadn't known were done. She questioned him about those.

He replied, "It's in the male manual. You recall, you believed I had a different one? You were correct. The female one is different and slanted as to gender."

"Baloney."

"A meat product. You are hungered? This is not the noon hour. Nor the supper hour. You are hungered for the *s-e-x?*"

She sputtered.

After that he just said, "Do not interrupt." And he had his wily way with her.

When they were spent and lay in a heap of inert-
ness, he said, "An energy that should be tapped. It is
dissipated."

"So'm I."

In his own voice, he asked softly, "Aren't you
ashamed of yourself for acting so quickly? Have you
so little faith in me?"

"I was jealous."

"How could you be?"

"Only three days ago, you were going to spend the
evening in mourning."

He sighed hugely, and his voice became alien. "I
hadn't met you yet. How was I to know that when I
landed on this planet, you would be here? You're
supposed to be on Orion in the body of a wasp-waisted
flea."

"Ugh."

"With long eyelashes."

"I have never in my life been jealous."

His voice reverted. "Before now."

"Before now."

"You have no cause."

"You got right up and went to her."

"She's an old acquaintance. Had I ignored her, you
would have considered me crass."

And she knew that he was right. She would tell him
so, some other time.

He said it again, but he elaborated. "You have no
cause to be jealous of any woman in all this universe.
I love you, Margot Pulver. You're going to marry me,
once you become adjusted to the idea, and we're going to live happily ever after, being tolerant and kind
to other people, too."

He meant they would be kind to each other first. She had not been kind to him or to Lucilla, who had once been named Priscilla. She sighed and said "I know," but she made the tone disgruntled enough that she could get away with saying it and not appear to have given up.

"Let me give you a shower."

"Not yet."

"You're jealous *and* selfish. Do you have other flaws?"

She readily replied, "Yes."

"What a lot of work you're going to be. How come your parents left all the smoothing up to me? They were careless. They should have sent you to Salty and Felicia when you were younger, and I could have worked on your sexual development at that time."

"You have complaints about my making love?"

"You hesitate to touch me as if I'll bite."

She giggled. She slithered up his lax body and peered into his eyes. "Is the alien gone?"

"What alien?"

"Do you remember making love to me?"

"When?"

"Just now."

He gasped in obvious shock. "Do you mean you used my body without even asking me?"

"Yes."

"How was I?"

"Marvelous."

"Good," he said. "Let's go shower and get dressed. It's almost suppertime."

"What happened to lunch?"

"We've wakened under a different schedule. The house had lunch hours ago, while you were toying with my body. You probably never even heard the chime ring.''

"No," she agreed.

"A late breakfast and then a skipped lunch. We've not been scheduled well. What will the staff think of us?''

"Only of you. Your room is still neat and orderly. They'll speculate on whose bed you've occupied.''

"I told them, in case there were any calls.''

She was appalled!

"Was it a secret?'' he asked in some surprise.

"A discreet secret.''

"Oh. I hadn't known. I thought since Lemon said he wasn't a contender for you, it wouldn't matter about where we were or how.''

"I told you I came here to meet you.''

"A man picks a woman like an apple picks a farmer.''

"Does that terrify you?''

"You did say we've already made love?''

"Mmm-hmm.''

"Then you'd better get your soft, salacious body off of my naked, vulnerable one, or we could miss supper, too.''

Eventually, they did get downstairs and in time for supper. But at the long table, while she was on John's right, at the foot of the table, Lucilla was on his left.

Margot's cheeks were pinkened with her unease and hostility, but she sat down with no comment. She spoke to the man to her right and was busy with eating and replied with an occasional word to John.

John kicked her shin!

She flared her eyes and stared at him. He smiled nicely and said, "Lucilla was asking about your sisters."

And her eyes glanced at Lucilla without her permission.

Lucilla was beautiful. She was perfectly made-up and her hair was exact, but in such a way that a man wouldn't be intimidated about mussing it up.

Lucilla smiled slightly and said to the younger woman, "I know your older sisters. I always envied them. I was an only child. They laughed so together. They always had such fun. I could never manage to capture their attention. I wanted so to share their companionship, but they didn't need anyone else."

And Margot was tongue-tied. This magic woman was envious of her sisters, who had been envious of her! How ironic! Margot replied, "They thought you were so beautiful and so poised that you didn't need them."

Lucilla shook her head ruefully. "We all need other people."

Those around their end of the table had listened and added comments of their own. They spoke of friendship and envy and of wanting to be a part of other peoples' lives.

Margot couldn't believe the need they all expressed. And she realized how fortunate she had been in her close family, of having the family protection that she had taken for granted. The sharing. The harbor they were.

John said, "That's the way it is with the Browns up in Temple, Ohio, where I grew up."

And Margot saw family closeness was something they shared.

The old rules were still observed in some places. The ladies left the table to the men and went into a drawing room where liqueurs were served. And even then, some of the ladies still smoked.

Lucilla sought Margot, and they spoke together. Lucilla said, "I know why you rode the pinto. But you have no cause to be concerned about me. John loves you."

"He made love with you." Margot was vulnerable.

Lucilla's eyes were gentle, and they held a trace of sadness. "Actually, no. We had sex."

"He has a great nostalgia about you. He suffered."

"I'm older than he. I was his first affair. A great convenience. It was only a crush. He is such a gentleman that he felt he should love me because I—accommodated him. It wasn't that serious."

"You didn't love him?"

"There was no one else, at the time. He was dear and charming. He plays a wonderful game of bridge. He rides well. He was a marvelous escort."

"If you didn't care for him, why did you...use him for that while?"

"I introduced him to Lemon. John and I have known each other, casually, for some years. We fell into the affair gradually. As I said, it was one of convenience. He hadn't met you, as yet."

"He couldn't SEE me because of you."

"He is an old-fashioned man, and he felt responsible for me because I was...his convenience. Lemon said you loved John, so I broke off with him. You are very suited to one another. And he loves you."

"In this brief time?"

"Oddly, yes." Lucilla smiled so gently, and there was the sadness that lay behind her eyes.

Lucilla was so gracious and so gentle that Margot felt as if she were twelve and finally allowed in with the adults.

The men came into the room, and John came instantly to Margot. He smiled at Lucilla and kissed her cheek. "Isn't she just as I said?"

Lucilla laughed with real humor and told Margot, "I told him you were perfect over a year ago. Now he claims all the credit for finding you."

Lucilla's statement whirled rather oddly in Margot's head, making her a little bit dizzy. She blinked.

John asked Lucilla, "Will you excuse us? I have to show Margot something in the library."

Margot's feet moved as John took her arm and tugged it a little toward the drawing-room door. He made their excuses as he smiled, and he led Margot out the door.

In the hall, she protested, pulling away, but he bent down, put her over his shoulder and carried her to the library.

They went inside, and John locked the door. It was something like coming full circle. As he stood her back on her feet, she asked, "What are we doing here?"

"I had Fred bring us some brandy and some of his best cookies. I just wanted to talk to you and not share you with anyone else."

"Lucilla is a lady."

John smiled a benediction on her.

"I suspect she has the morals of an alley cat, but she hides it very well."

He sighed with forbearance, gave her an excessively patient look to boot as he said, "Your progress is snail pace."

She looked around everywhere in his direction without ever actually looking at him. She appeared to be patient and tolerant. She licked her bottom lip as if she had something stuck on it, and she couldn't think of anything of interest to say.

"Your restraint is obvious."

She smiled at him.

"Come. I haven't yet moved Adam's fig leaf. Since you discovered that it moved, I've been curious."

"You can manage it."

"I want to know why you laughed."

"Go look."

He tugged her arm. "I want to see you move the leaf."

"If I do that, then you'll want me to move yours."

The air went out of his lungs and he wilted a little as he put a supporting hand to his bent forehead. "You're a menace to a man who is trying to be careful."

"Be CAREFUL? Be careful! You want me to go move Adam's fig leaf and you call that being *careful?*"

"Okay. I'll do it myself."

So she sat on the sofa, and he went over and investigated Adam's fig leaf. There was another fig leaf exactly the same size painted under the movable one. He said, "How juvenile."

She said, "You looked. Who is juvenile?"

"We're back where we started."

They considered one another. She said, "We're different people than we were just three days ago."

"I wasn't in love with you then."

"I knew you were in this room. I followed you."

"You belched and scratched."

She explained with logic, "I wanted you to believe my surprise when I allowed myself to 'see' you."

"Come upstairs to my room."

"No. I think we need some time apart to evaluate this phenomenon."

"The day is done." He picked her up off the couch and carried her quite easily. Some men are stronger than others.

She inquired flippantly, "Is this some of your admitted unreasonable behavior?"

"Not yet, but you're getting closer." He took her to his room and removed all of her clothing with care and relish. Then he made improper love to her. He took a long time and he was very thorough. And when they were replete, he lay his hand on her and said, "Now you can tell me that you love me."

And she said, "Yes."

Having been raised in similar circumstances, Margot wasn't overwhelmed by the extended Brown family. She fit in as if she'd stepped onto a familiar conveyor belt.

The marriage between Margot and John that summer was a doubled family reunion, and the primary couple had only brief attentions in the crush of the guests. The bridal couple did attract the majority briefly as they were wed and as they departed for their honeymoon.

But the party went on into the next day. The Pulvers and the Browns were well matched.

As for the cause of their families' successful melding, the two honeymooners took three days to adjust to being alone and legal. They smiled and touched and laughed out loud.

And they lived happily ever after.

* * * * *

Take 4 bestselling love stories FREE

Plus get a FREE surprise gift!

SOMETHING WILD

As seen on TV!
Free Gift Offer

With a Free Gift proof-of-purchase from any Silhouette® book,
you can receive a beautiful cubic zirconia pendant.

This gorgeous marquise-shaped stone is a genuine cubic
zirconia—accented by an 18" gold tone necklace.

(Approximate retail value $19.95)

Send for yours today...
compliments of ▼ *Silhouette*®
TM

Free Gift Certificate

Name: _____

Address: _____

City: _____ State/Province: _____ Zip/Postal Code: _____

079-KBZ